## "Where are we going?"

"We're going to see your sister's old boyfriend. I intend to beat the rest of the truth out of him and then we're calling the sheriff."

That look—the one like a wild animal trapped in the headlights of an oncoming car—claimed her face, filled Cece's eyes. "You believe me?"

Before he could stop himself, Deacon grabbed her face in his hands and kissed her. He hadn't meant to. Definitely had not meant to kiss her so hard and so deeply. Her lips felt so soft beneath his. Her skin so smooth and delicate in his palms. Every cell in his body started to burn. Her fingers touched his hands, trembled, and he wanted to pull her beneath him and do things she would hate him for when this was finished.

When he could control himself once more, he drew his mouth from hers, but he could not let go...could not lose that contact. He pressed his forehead to hers. Closed his eyes and reached for reason.

But there was no reason.

Not in this.

# THE STRANGER NEXT DOOR

USA TODAY Bestselling Author

## DEBRA WEBB

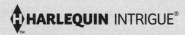
HARLEQUIN INTRIGUE®

This book is dedicated to my brothers and sister.
Thanks for being my family!

ISBN-13: 978-1-335-60452-1

The Stranger Next Door

Copyright © 2019 by Debra Webb

PLEASE RECYCLE
THIS PRODUCT IS RECYCLABLE

Recycling programs
for this product may
not exist in your area.

Printed in U.S.A.

**Debra Webb** is the award-winning *USA TODAY* bestselling author of more than one hundred novels, including those in reader-favorite series Faces of Evil, the Colby Agency and the Shades of Death. With more than four million books sold in numerous languages and countries, Debra has a love of storytelling that goes back to childhood on a farm in Alabama. Visit Debra at www.debrawebb.com.

## Books by Debra Webb

### Harlequin Intrigue

#### A Winchester, Tennessee Thriller

*In Self Defense*
*The Dark Woods*
*The Stranger Next Door*

#### Colby Agency: Sexi-ER

*Finding the Edge*
*Sin and Bone*
*Body of Evidence*

#### Faces of Evil

*Dark Whispers*
*Still Waters*

#### Colby Agency: The Specialists

*Bridal Armor*
*Ready, Aim...I Do!*

### Colby, TX

*Colby Law*
*High Noon*
*Colby Roundup*

### Debra Webb writing with Regan Black

#### Harlequin Intrigue

#### Colby Agency: Family Secrets

*Gunning for the Groom*

#### The Specialists: Heroes Next Door

*The Hunk Next Door*
*Heart of a Hero*
*To Honor and To Protect*
*Her Undercover Defender*

# CAST OF CHARACTERS

**Cecelia Winters**—After eight years in prison for a murder she didn't commit, Cece wants just one thing: to find the truth.

**Special Agent Deacon Ross**—He's on a mission. One he has put everything on hold to finish. But will the truth he finds be the one he's looking for?

**Jack Kemp**—He's been missing for more than eight years. It's time someone paid for what happened to him.

**Levi Winters**—He wants to help his sister Cece, but will he get himself killed doing so?

**Marcus Winters**—The only thing he wants is for Cece to go away.

**Sierra Winters**—She will never reveal her secrets.

# Chapter One

Murderer. Cecelia Winters stared at the ugly word scrawled in red paint across the white front door. She glanced back at the taxi that was already speeding away down the dusty road. She sighed, dropped her backpack onto the porch.

Her brother Levi was supposed to have picked her up at the prison when she was released. Evidently something had held him up. She went up on her tiptoes but still could not reach the ledge above the door. Surveying the porch, she decided a chair would work for what she needed. The two ladder-back chairs and the swing had been a part of her grandmother's front porch for as long as Cecelia could remember. The wicker plant stand that stood between the chairs was empty and in serious need of painting. Tiny flakes of faded white paint lay on the floor around it.

"Falling apart like everything else around here,"

she grumbled as she dragged the chair to the door and climbed atop it.

The key lay on the dusty ledge just as it always had. It would be a flat-out miracle if the house hadn't been vandalized and cleaned out of anything worth taking. But Cece, as she had always been called, wasn't complaining. Her grandmother had left her this old house with the ten acres that surrounded it. The walls were still standing and the roof appeared in reasonably good condition. Anything over and above that would be icing on the cake. Cece was enormously thankful to have a place to stay at all. What was left of her family had turned their backs on her a long time ago.

Except for her grandmother, her momma's momma. She had never believed the lies. And Cece's little brother—at least, she had thought her brother had not turned on her. He had not shown up to pick her up when she was released so she could not be certain. Last month he had visited her at the prison. He had seemed fine and, frankly, over the moon that she would soon be free.

No one was happier about that than Cece. She had served her time.

She stared at the red letters of the word painted on the door once more before opening it and stepping inside. No matter that it was barely two in the afternoon, gloom filled the house that had always been Cece's refuge growing up. The shades, she realized. Moving from window to window, she tugged gently on the old roller-style shades, causing each one to slide upward and allowing sunlight into the house. Dust floated in the air, filtering through the rays of light like a thousand miniscule snowflakes in an old snow globe with yellowed glass.

Emily Broward had died one year ago. The house had sat empty, awaiting its new owner's release from prison. Levi had sworn he had checked in on things from time to time but Cece could not be sure he had done so. The house was neat and clean—other than the dust—so she supposed he had dropped by on occasion. Her grandmother had been an immaculate housekeeper, so the neatness wasn't surprising and likely had nothing to do with Levi's drive-bys.

The house was small. A living room, eat-in kitchen, two bedrooms and a bath. There was an attic and a tiny brick-walled and stone-floored basement that was more a root cellar than anything else. The house was plenty roomy enough, her grandmother had always said. The furniture was the same as Cece remembered from her childhood. Emily Broward had been far too frugal to spend money on new furniture when what she had remained serviceable.

Which, Cece imagined, was how she had hung on to what was left of this small family farm for nearly half a century. Emily's one and only child, a daughter and Cece's mother, had died more than twenty years ago. So the place now belonged to Cece. In truth, if not for this house, she would never have come back to the Winchester area. She had sworn she wouldn't be back. Ever.

But here she was.

Really, what else could she do? She had nothing but

the clothes on her back and the backpack she'd had with her when she'd been arrested nearly nine years ago. She had nothing. No money. No job. No family— unless you counted her no-show younger brother, the sole sibling who hadn't disowned her.

Still, there was the matter of the truth. No matter that she had told herself a thousand times that she did not care, she did. Somewhere in this town, someone knew the truth and she wanted to find it. To prove she was not a cold-blooded murderer. To show whoever cared that she was the good girl her grandmother Emily always believed her to be.

Pushing away the overwhelming and painful thoughts, Cece decided what she needed at this moment was paint. Didn't matter what color. Anything to smear over the ugly word slashed across the front door.

Paint and tools were in the old smokehouse. Her grandmother had stopped using the smokehouse for its original purpose years ago, after Cece's grandfather passed away. She had turned it into a gardening shed. Flower and vegetable gardening had been Emily's favorite thing in the world.

Cece headed out the back door. The smaller rear porch was a little less stable than the front. South facing, it weathered the harshest elements. She would need to have a closer look at its condition soon. Her grandmother had been one of those women who refused to be helpless in any way. She had learned how to wield a hammer and a shotgun with equal skill. Cece would just have to do the same since she had no resources.

But first, she would need a job.

She opened the door to the smokehouse and peered into the dark interior. She shuddered, wondered if her grandmother's shotgun was still in the same place. Probably in her closet or under the bed. Deep breath. She stepped inside, reaching overhead for the string that would turn on the light. Her fingers found it and she pulled. The bare bulb glared to life, spilling light over the dusty, cobweb-infested space.

It took some doing but she found an old bucket of white paint. When she had opened it, removed a hard skin from over the top and vigorously stirred the contents, it appeared to be enough for her purposes. Hopefully.

With a serviceable brush rounded up, she turned off the light and closed up the smokehouse. There was a good deal of cleanup she needed to do. Someone had been keeping the yard cut, which was a really good thing. Augusts were generally as hot as Hades and rain was typically scarce. Snakes would be actively searching for water sources. About the only thing she disliked more than snakes were spiders. Banishing the idea of creepy, crawly things, Cece scrubbed a coat of paint over the graffiti. It would take several coats to cover the red, or maybe she would have to pick up a stain-blocking product to help make the glaring reality go away.

*You need money for that, Cece.*

After cleaning the brush and pressing the lid back onto the paint can, she decided to have a look in the bedroom she had used before ending up in prison. She left the front door ajar with its wet paint and headed that way. Her father had kicked her out of the house when she was sixteen. At the time she had been only too happy to go. She wouldn't have stayed that long if not for her younger sister. She had worried about Sierra, who was four years younger, but she had learned the hard way that her little sister was quite capable of taking care of herself.

Her grandmother had warned her, but Cece had not wanted to see it. Sierra had turned into a selfish, belligerent teenager. As a little kid she had looked up to Cece. Hung onto her hand every chance she got. Crawled into bed with her when she was scared. They had both been so young when their mother died, but especially Sierra. She had only been two years old. Cece had tried to be more than just a big sister. Fat lot of good it had done her.

Sierra and Marcus, their older brother, were fanatical just like their father had been. According to Levi, Marcus had taken over her father's church—cult was a better description. And Sierra was his right hand.

Another reason Cece would rather have been anywhere than here.

Regardless of how she pretended, she could not leave. Not until she found the truth. In the final letter she had received from her grandmother before Emily passed away, she had told Cece that her trusted attorney, Clarence Frasier, had hired a private investigator to help find the truth.

Unfortunately Frasier had died two months ago without passing along any new developments in the investigation. His partner had sent her a letter saying he would not be able to pursue her case or represent her. Her file was available for pickup should she choose to do so. Additionally, in his letter, he had confirmed her fears about the private investigator's inability to find anything new.

Probably she would pick up the files in a day or two. For now, she just wanted to be alone and enjoy being outside those gray prison walls. A nice hot bath or shower in private was very high on her list. Planning her own menu and picking out what she would wear. No one realized how important all those little decisions were until the right to make them was taken away.

The clothes she had owned before she was arrested still hung in the closet. Underthings and pajamas were neatly folded in drawers—her grandmother's doing, no doubt. Cece had never been that organized. Her heart squeezed at the memory of how she had begged to be allowed to visit her grandmother in the hospital those final days of her life and, when Emily was gone, to be able to attend her funeral. Cece's persistence had landed her in isolation for a week.

She would visit the cemetery soon. Take flowers, as soon as she had money to purchase something nice.

At the dresser, she hesitated before turning away. A framed photo of her mother and her grandmother from twenty-five years ago captured her attention. Cece had the same curly red hair as her mother and her grandmother. She was the only one in the family to inherit the red hair and green eyes. Marcus and Levi had dark brown hair with brown eyes, like their father. Sierra's hair was even darker, as were her eyes. Her coloring was a fact Cece's father had held against her. He had sworn her red hair was the mark of the devil. She remembered him telling her mother the same thing. Her mother had died when Cece was six years old but she remembered those cruel words.

Her father had been a mean man, and harsh, hurtful words and actions were the only memories Cece had of him. She hoped he was burning in hell.

Her grandmother would pat her on the hand and assure her he was, indeed, roasting in hell. She had hated Mason Winters. Her daughter's—her only child's—marriage to him had broken her heart.

Cece shook off the painful memories. There was a lot she needed to do. Starting with stocking the kitchen. Though food wasn't exactly a priority for her, she had to eat. The attorney had said in his letter that a credit of five hundred dollars awaited her at the market in town. Frasier's doing, no doubt. He had felt sorry for Cece and had adored her grandmother. Cece had often wondered if he had been in love with her grandmother. He had certainly seemed to be. He had been a widower, she a widow, but to Cece's knowledge their relationship had never been anything other than friendship.

Cece closed the front door and locked it. She tucked the key into the pocket of her jeans and went to the kitchen to see if her grandmother had still kept her truck keys in the drawer by the back door. She pulled the drawer open and there they were. She snatched up the keys and headed out to the side of the barn her grandparents had used as a garage. She raised the crossbar and the double doors swung open. She climbed into the blue truck that was twice as old as she was and inserted the key.

She said a quick prayer in hopes that Levi had done as he had promised and kept the truck in running order. Her grandparents had maintained it in immaculate condition, but after Emily's death the battery would have died if the truck wasn't started regularly, driven around a bit. Levi had promised to drive it once a week until Cece came home.

Holding her breath, she turned the key and pumped the accelerator.

The engine purred to life as if she had just driven the vehicle off the showroom floor.

Relieved, she slid the gearshift into Reverse and backed out of the garage. Her grandmother had taught her to close the garage doors whenever she took the truck anywhere. No one who passed would realize she was gone as long as those doors were closed. Even in a small town, run-of-the-mill thieves could be found.

Far worse could be found, as well. The really bad ones just knew how to hide better than the others.

THE DRIVE TO Ollie's in Winchester took scarcely twenty minutes. The first few miles were easy. Driving was like riding a bike, her grandmother had said in her letters. You won't forget how whether you haven't driven for eight years or eighty. She had been right about that part.

But the traffic—even in a small town—had Cece's heart pounding, her fingers gripping the steering wheel and sweat beading on her forehead. The fact that it was ninety-five degrees did not help. The old truck didn't have any climate control features. Her grandfather had insisted the windows were control enough. *You either let the climate in or you do not,* he would say.

All the noise—from the many different sounds blowing in through her window to the other vehicles on the road—had Cece on edge, as well. Not that she was complaining. It would just take some getting used to.

Cece did not breathe easy until she had braked to a stop in the lot at the market and thrust the gearshift into Park. For good measure, she engaged the emergency brake before climbing out. She pocketed the keys but didn't bother locking the doors since there was nothing in the truck worth stealing. The bench seat was a little on the worn side and the rubber-coated floorboards had never been covered with mats as far as she recalled. Just a plain old truck. No rust or dents but very basic. The automatic transmission was the one upgrade, and that had been added only because her grandmother pitched a fit about it back when her grandfather decided to buy a truck.

The asphalt steamed as she crossed to the store entrance. With only a handful of cars in the lot, she was hopeful that she wouldn't run into anyone who remembered her. Eight years was a long time. If she were lucky most folks would have forgotten her by now.

Yeah, right. Like people forgot when a girl was charged with murdering her father.

She would never live that down—no matter that she was innocent.

Her fingers curled around the handle of the shopping cart and she started with the aisle closest to the entrance. The store looked different now. At some point over the years it had been remodeled and she had no clue where anything was anymore, but she would leave empty-handed before she asked for help and drew attention to herself.

Mostly she only needed the basics. Bread, milk, cheese, eggs. Maybe some peanut butter and crackers. The fruit department spread out before her and she decided fruit would be nice, as well. She grabbed apples, berries, oranges and bananas before stopping to think that she had no idea how much this stuff cost anymore. Since she only had a limited amount of credit, she had to be careful.

Keeping the apples and bananas, she put the berries and oranges back and moved on. Next time she would have those. When she reached the coffee aisle, she realized she could not live without a caffeine fix every morning. Since her grandmother had preferred hot tea and only bought instant coffee for guests, there was no coffee maker. Cece grabbed a jar of instant and moved on. Resisting the snack aisle, she strolled on to the dairy department. When she had mentally checked off the items on her list and deposited each one into her cart, she headed for the checkout counter.

Fortunately, the cashier was young, maybe seventeen or eighteen. She wouldn't know Cece.

When she had rung up the final item, she looked at Cece. "That'll be sixty-two fifty-eight."

Uncertainty seared through her. How did she explain the credit? "Is there a manager on duty?"

The girl stared at Cece, impatience written all over her face. "Sure." She called for the manager over the loudspeaker.

Cece ignored the people who glanced at the register and her. What if the manager on duty had no idea about the credit? Her stomach twisted into a thousand knots. She should have called the attorney's office before coming here.

"She has a question," the cashier said, yanking Cece's attention to the man who approached the checkout.

He was older, fifty or so, and looked vaguely familiar. Tension banded around her chest making a breath near impossible. When he frowned, her anxiety escalated.

"Cece?"

She nodded, the move jerky.

A smile propped up the corners of his mouth. "Make a note of the amount," he said to the cashier. "The lady has a credit that will take care of the total." To Cece he said, "Whenever you come in, just have them write the total and my name on the back of the receipt and tuck it into the till."

Cece searched her memory banks but his name was lost to her.

"Thanks, Mr. Holland," the cashier said, saving Cece from having to ask.

She nodded. "Yes, thank you."

Holland sent her an answering nod and returned to whatever he had been doing before the cashier had summoned him to the front.

By the time the cashier had written Holland on the

back of the receipt and deposited it into the till, a short line had formed behind Cece. She had her bags in her cart and was ready to run a good five seconds before the girl glanced at her and said the words that would allow her to feel comfortable making her exit, "Thanks. Come again."

Cece was almost to the door when a female voice called out behind her, "Aren't you that girl who killed her daddy?"

Cece did not look back, just kept going. Her focus narrowed to the old blue truck waiting for her in the parking lot. All she had to do was reach that truck, load her stuff into the passenger seat and drive away. When she had money of her own, she would go to Tullahoma or some other nearby town where people were less likely to know her. Then again, even if she had had money, the fear of her driving skills being too rusty would have kept her close to home today.

She remembered well how it was here—the way it was in most small towns—news of her return would rush along the gossip grapevine like a fire devouring dry leaves. Passenger-side door open, she placed her bags in the seat and floorboard. With the task complete, she ordered herself to breathe.

*Slow, deep breath.* She was okay. She would be in the truck and on her way in a minute. This first foray into public was nearly over.

For a second she considered leaving the shopping cart sitting in the middle of the lot, but the manager had been nice to her, and she shouldn't repay him by leaving the cart where it might hit a parked vehicle or roll out onto the street and cause an accident. Besides, the cart corral was only a few steps away. The clash of metal as she slid the cart into the line of others already in there made her cringe. She wasn't sure when the fear that someone would attack her would diminish. Learning to be on guard at all times was necessary to survival in prison. Many things had been necessary to survival—things she wanted to forget.

"Murderer!"

Cece turned around to face the woman who shouted at her…a different one from the voice that had called out to her in the store.

This woman wasn't alone.

Cece's heart stuttered. Three women and four—no, five—men spread out between Cece and her truck. She didn't know any of them, but she recognized the clothes they wore. Plain, overly modest, drab in color. Salvation Survivalists. Members of her father's following. She refused to call it a church. These people had nothing to do with God.

"We shall purge this evil from our midst!" one of the men shouted.

Cece stood perfectly still. If she ran they would only chase her. If she called out for help she would be wasting her time since there was no one to hear her.

The woman who had spoken first drew back her right arm and flung something at Cece. It struck her in the side, making her flinch at the sharp pain, before bouncing onto the asphalt.

*Rock?*

Memories of rocks being thrown at a helpless woman whispered through her mind.

Another rock flew at her. Hit her shoulder.

She backed up, bumped into the line of carts.

"Stone her for her grievous sin!" one of the men shouted.

Cece turned to run. She had no choice. Stones hit her back, her legs, her shoulder. When one hit her on the head, she bit her lip to prevent crying out.

Before she could take off running, a man blocked her path. Tall, dark hair...dark eyes.

She opened her mouth to scream.

He grabbed her and pulled her behind him.

"Back off," he growled at the mob. "The police are on the way. Unless one or all of you wants to be arrested, you had better get the hell out of here."

Cece dared to peek beyond one broad shoulder. The stones had stopped flying but the group still stood there lurking like something from a bad horror movie.

"We're not finished," the woman who had spoken first said, her hate-filled gaze on Cece.

The siren in the distance had the group dispersing.

Cece watched as they climbed into two SUVs and sped away. The woman—the one who appeared to be in charge—stared at Cece as they drove away.

The woman's face didn't trigger any memories, but she certainly knew Cece.

The idea that they had all come together suggested that the attack against her had been planned. Anger, hurt and frustration twisted inside her.

"You all right?"

Cece looked at the man who had come to her rescue and nodded. She wanted to ask his name. She wanted to ask why he had come to her aid. But she couldn't seem to put the words together and force them beyond her lips.

The Winchester Police Department cruiser came to a rocking stop a few feet away and Cece was grateful the stranger took the initiative and explained the incident to the officer. By this time Mr. Holland had come out to the parking lot.

"Are you okay?" he asked Cece.

"Yes." She relaxed the tiniest bit.

The police officer approached her then. "Miss Winters, would you like to come to the station and fill out a report?"

Cece shook her head. "I just want to go home, please."

Holland turned to the officer. "I think that's a good idea. She's had enough excitement for today."

The officer nodded. "I'll let Chief Brannigan know you're home, Miss Winters. He'll check in on you. Be sure to let us know if you have any more trouble. The chief doesn't tolerate nonsense like this."

Cece found the wherewithal to thank him.

"I'll follow her home. Make sure she gets unloaded without any trouble."

She stared at the stranger. Why would a man she had never met go out of his way?

"Good idea, Ross," the officer said. He turned to Cece. "Miss Winters, Mr. Ross lives just down the road from you. He bought the old Wilburn place."

The Wilburns. She remembered them. "I'm sure I'll be okay now, Mr. Ross." She met the stranger's gaze. "Thank you for your help."

All she wanted to do was get into her truck and drive away. Before anyone could attempt to change her mind, she rushed to her truck and climbed in. She left without looking back. She made it all the way to the city limits before the tears defeated her. She swiped at her eyes, frustrated and angry…mostly at herself.

She was back, and by God she was not going to be run out of this damned town until she had the truth.

## Chapter Two

Deacon Ross stood at the edge of the woods, watching the house. Cecelia Winters had carried in her supplies a couple of bags at a time. She had not purchased all that much. Her funds were limited. He suspected the attorney—Frasier—had made some sort of arrangements before his untimely death.

It seemed that no matter how guilty most folks in the town thought Cecelia was, there were a few who wanted to look out for her best interests. The attorney he could understand—that was his job and he had been an old friend of her grandmother's. The chief of police and the county sheriff going out of their way to keep her safe infuriated Deacon, but, like the attorney, that was their job.

Chief of Police Brannigan and Sheriff Tanner had taken extraordinary measures to ensure no one learned the date she was coming home. If it had not been for Deacon putting the word out, she would have reappeared in Winchester with no fanfare at all.

He could not allow that to happen.

Fury fired through him. Made him flinch with its intensity.

The murder of her old man wasn't the only crime Cecelia Winters had committed. Another man, a man who meant a great deal to Deacon, had disappeared around the time of that murder. It had taken years to narrow down the possibilities, but a year ago Deacon had discovered reason to believe Cece was involved. He had been digging into her past and her family since. If it was the last thing he accomplished in this life, he intended to find out what she knew about his friend's disappearance. As the date for her release from prison neared he had reached an important conclusion: the only way to find the facts he needed was to get close to her.

Eight years, seven months and nineteen days had passed since her arrest and she had not once changed her story. She was innocent, she claimed. She had not killed her father. When her appeals were exhausted, she quietly served out her time. Due to the circumstances surrounding her childhood, the judge had been lenient in his sentencing. The crime that should have earned her twenty years had garnered her only eight.

But the disappearance—probable murder—of Deacon's partner would be a different story. If she had played any role in his death, he intended to see that she was charged, found guilty and sentenced to the fullest extent allowed for that heartless crime. More of that fury ignited deep in his gut.

Jack Kemp had been a good man. A good man as well as Deacon's mentor and partner. Deacon blamed himself in part for not being here to provide backup for Jack. But the Bureau had wanted one of them to stay on the case in Gallatin. The investigation there had been on the verge of busting wide open. In the end, half a dozen people had died in Gallatin—all part of the extreme survivalist cult known as Resurrection. Since he disappeared, Jack had not been able to prove it but he'd believed the survivalists in Gallatin were connected to the ones in the Winchester area. The church—more a cult than a church—the Salvation Survivalists, was somehow serving as a liaison between the two branches.

All those years ago, Jack's investigation had been buried under a mountain of red tape. The powers that be hadn't wanted to acknowledge that Resurrection's reach was so wide and deep. The information had been suppressed for years. Deacon wondered if the truth would have ever come to light if he had not pushed so hard for so long. Jack's family had a right to know what happened to him. Deacon intended to see that he or his body was found and the mystery surrounding his disappearance was solved.

The death of Mason Winters nearly nine years ago had caused the group to close ranks even tighter. In all this time, no one had gotten close to infiltrating the group and several had tried. Despite the Bureau's attempt to conceal what went wrong with Jack and his investigation, they continued to tap any resource that could be found. Except, in Deacon's opinion, they were looking in all the wrong places.

Now he had a loose thread at ground zero—Cecelia Winters. He would learn all her secrets as quickly as possible. Time was not on his side. If she knew things, as he suspected she did, someone would tie up that loose end. *Soon.*

She knew what had really happened. He was certain of it. She was a part of the family Jack had been investigating. She was the only one who had the proper motivation to tell the truth. Her family had turned on her, which gave her every reason to no longer have any loyalty to them. Deacon would find the truth before he was finished here, no matter how long it took and no matter what he had to do to make it happen.

Everything had been set in motion. All he had to do now was watch and take advantage of the opportunities to get close to her. The people in this community who despised her would take care of the rest. Cecelia Winters had no idea how much her father's followers hated her. She had killed their messiah, their leader. Those who rose to power after his death were even more heinous—particularly her brother Marcus.

Before this was over she would wish a thousand times she had stayed in that hellhole of a prison. She would want to run—to get away from the past that haunted her. But she wasn't going anywhere until Deacon had what he'd come for.

He turned away from her and walked back through the stretch of woods that separated the place he had bought from the one she had inherited. He'd set up a stand of trees near her house so that he could watch her. Anyone who stumbled upon it would believe it was a hunter's blind. Hunting season was still a way off but hard-core hunters started prepping early.

When he reached the clearing in front of his house, he hesitated. A truck had pulled into his driveway. A moment or so later, the driver emerged. He crossed the yard and climbed the porch steps.

Sheriff Colt Tanner.

Deacon skirted the rear yard and headed for the back door. He had no idea why Tanner would visit him. Maybe to follow up on the incident in the Ollie's parking lot. Deacon had given a statement. He didn't see the need for additional questioning. But the sheriff had been somewhat skeptical of him since his move to the Winchester area. No surprise there. The man had good instincts.

Following the disappearance of his partner, Deacon had been ordered to stay away from the investigation. He had been forced to do his digging quietly and under the radar of his superiors. The decision made no sense to him. He should have been the one ferreting out the facts about Jack. The Bureau had not seen it that way. Too personal, they had argued. Deacon was ordered to leave Winchester and to keep his nose out of the investigation. He had done as he was told—until one year ago. When the case had been closed, his partner legally declared dead.

Deacon had started his own off-the-record investigation. In Winchester, Logan Wilburn had gotten himself murdered and his property had gone on the market. Deacon had bought it sight unseen only because the closest neighbor was the mini farm Cecelia had inherited.

With those steps in place, Deacon had taken a leave of absence from the Bureau and moved here to set up his cover. He had learned who was who, burrowed into the community, and then he had waited. But Colt Tanner had kept a wary eye on him.

He imagined that was what this visit was about, more so than the nasty mob at Ollie's.

As Deacon moved through the house, a firm knock echoed in the living room, most likely the second one since the sheriff's arrival. Deacon tossed his hat onto the side table near the door, unlocked and opened it.

"Sheriff," he said by way of a greeting.

"Ross," Tanner replied. "You have a few minutes?"

"Sure. Come on in." Deacon opened the door wide and waited for the other man to step inside.

Tanner paused in the center of the living room and removed his hat. "You've done a lot of work around this old place."

Deacon closed the door and faced him. "Not so much." He glanced around. "Paint mostly. Some maintenance that had gone by the wayside."

"Looks good."

Most of what Deacon had done around the place had been merely a part of building his cover. A necessary phase in establishing credibility. "I'm sure you didn't drop by to check out my DIY skills. How can I help you, sheriff?"

"First, I want to reiterate how much Chief Brannigan and I appreciate you stepping in to help Miss Winters today."

Brannigan had already said as much. Deacon was fairly confident this visit wasn't just so Tanner could pass along his appreciation in person, as well. "It was the neighborly thing to do."

Tanner held his white hat in his hands. Like the rest of the men in power around here, he sported a cowboy hat, boots and well-worn jeans. Deacon had chosen the same sort of attire, not because he actually considered himself a cowboy but because he wanted to fit in with the majority of the other "good" guys around the Winchester area. When Cecelia looked at him, he wanted her to see an image that reminded her of the sheriff or the chief. Someone she could trust.

Psychology 101. Play the part.

"Those folks were part of her dead daddy's church," Tanner said. "The whole group is up in arms. I don't know what part of the Bible they think makes it a Christian thing to do—going after a woman like that. I spoke to the leader, Marcus Winters, who is also Cece's brother. He's assured me there will be no more trouble but I don't trust him to follow through with that promise."

Deacon was well aware of who the people were. He was also thoroughly acquainted, if only secondhand, with the older brother. The man had stepped into his dead daddy's shoes as if he had planned the event. It was possible he and Cecelia had plotted the old man's murder together. Then again, the fact that Marcus and the younger sister, Sierra, had basically disowned Cecelia seemed to indicate otherwise.

Then there was the wild card, the younger brother, Levi. He had visited his sister in prison on a regular basis but then he had not picked her up when she was released. Had not dropped by since she arrived home.

"I'll do what I can to keep an eye out around here," Deacon said. Though he wasn't convinced the sheriff had paid him this visit to elicit his help in providing backup where the Winters woman was concerned.

"Do you know Cece's younger brother, Levi?"

The question surprised Deacon. "I know the name," he admitted. "I don't actually know him or any other member of her family." He shrugged. "I suppose I've seen him around."

"Strange," Tanner said. "About three weeks ago Levi caught me at home and went on and on about how he thought you might represent some threat to his sister. I asked him for details but he seemed reluctant to provide any."

Well, well. Levi had been watching him. Deacon had thought he'd spotted the man once but he hadn't been sure. Now he knew. Deacon shook his head. "I can't imagine where he got an idea like that, sheriff. I don't know his sister or him, beyond the rumors I've heard."

Tanner shifted his weight ever so slightly. "I took the liberty of running a background search on you, Ross. I hope you don't mind."

Deacon chuckled. "'Course not. I have nothing to

hide. I'm new in town. You have an obligation to the citizens of your county to look into potential trouble."

Tanner didn't comment on his reaction, apparently wasn't impressed or relieved. "You're an FBI agent. From Nashville. Not married. No family. What brought you to Winchester?"

"Real estate prices," Deacon said without hesitation. "Property in the Nashville area is crazy expensive. I was looking for a place to retire."

The sheriff was far from convinced. "You're thirty-five years old. Seems kind of young to be planning your retirement."

Deacon shook his head. "According to my investment counselor you're never too young to start preparing."

Tanner nodded. "Well, I guess there's some truth to that." He placed his hat on his head. "I suppose you'll be returning to Nashville eventually, considering that's where you're assigned. You must have had a hell of a lot of vacation days accrued."

Apparently the sheriff wasn't going to be happy with Deacon's glossed-over responses. "I requested a leave of absence. I'm not sure if I'll be returning to field duty."

Tanner studied him from beneath the brim of that white hat. "Is that right?"

"I hit a wall, sheriff. I'm certain you can understand how that can happen. I'm just not sure of what I want to do moving forward. Peace and quiet, for sure. Beyond that, I can't say." That was as close to the truth as he was going. But the basic story was accurate. Accurate enough to get him through this, he hoped.

"Law enforcement can take a toll. I hope you'll feel free to look me up if you need anything." Tanner chuckled. "Keep in mind, we're always on the lookout for experienced lawmen in the sheriff's department. If you're interested in coming on board, drop by and we'll talk."

"I'll keep that in mind, sheriff. Thank you. As for Levi Winters, if he still feels I represent some threat, I'm happy to meet with the two of you and hash out the issue."

Tanner nodded. "If I find him, I'll tell him. It's the strangest thing."

Deacon braced for whatever the sheriff intended to say next.

"I haven't been able to find him since that day. According to the warden at the prison no one showed up to give Cece a ride home. I recall that Levi said he would be picking her up. I'm surprised he didn't. He's the only one in her family who didn't turn on her during the trial."

"Have you spoken to Miss Winters to see if she's heard from him?"

"I was about to head over there now. A tech from the phone company is coming to turn on the landline. I called in a request as soon as I heard she was being released. I don't want her out here with no way to call for help. I doubt she has a cell phone yet."

"The service out here is not that great anyway," Deacon pointed out.

"All the more reason to go with a landline," Tanner agreed.

"Hold on, sheriff." Deacon rounded up a notepad and a pen. He scribbled his cell number on the top sheet, tore it off and passed it to the other man. "This is my cell number—for what it's worth. If she needs to call someone in the middle of the night, I'm closer than anyone else. I haven't bothered with a landline. Maybe I should."

"I'm sure she'll appreciate that, Ross." Tanner folded the paper and tucked it into his pocket.

He headed for the door. When he reached for the knob, Deacon added, "I was serious when I said if her brother wants to talk I'm more than willing. Just give me a call."

"Will do."

Tanner left and Deacon watched from the window as he loaded into his truck and drove away. The sheriff was friendly enough, but he wasn't completely satisfied with what he knew or what his instincts were telling him about Deacon. At the moment he had no reason to pursue the issue, but he would be watching and maybe doing a little more digging. Deacon wasn't concerned. The Bureau would not turn over information regarding an agent to anyone just to satisfy his curiosity. The only aspect of Deacon's past or present that could in any way be related to his being here was his former partner's disappearance, which had occurred a long time ago, and Deacon had not even been a part of that investigation.

Everything else he had told the sheriff could be confirmed with his direct supervisor if Tanner decided to push it that far.

Deacon waited a half hour or so, then he made his

way back through the woods, a path he knew well now, and watched her house. Tanner had gone inside and the technician from the telephone company had arrived and begun his work. For the next half hour or so the man went through the steps of running a line to the house and doing the necessary installation on the inside. Ten minutes after he left, Tanner did the same. Deacon walked back to his house and got into his truck. He backed out onto the road and drove the short distance to his neighbor's home.

He parked only a few yards from the porch steps. By the time he reached those steps she had already peeked through the curtain to identify her newest visitor. He pretended not to notice, walked to the door and knocked.

The sound of the locks disengaging and then the creak of the door echoed before her face appeared. "Yes?"

She recognized him; he saw it in her green eyes. Not to mention he doubted she would have opened the door if she hadn't.

"I'm your neighbor," he said, choosing to go that route rather than bring up what happened in the parking lot. "Deacon Ross."

She nodded. "Thank you for doing what you did today. I'm reasonably certain no one else would have."

"You don't need to thank me, Miss Winters. I did what needed to be done."

"I'm grateful." She glanced beyond him, then managed an uncertain smile. "I put your number on the wall by the phone. I hope I won't have to call you, but

I'll rest easier knowing there's someone I can." She shrugged. "I grew up here but I don't have any friends or…or family, none that still own me, anyway."

"I understand."

"I'm sorry." She backed up a couple of steps, opened the door wider. "I guess my manners are rusty. Would you like to come in?"

He had hoped she would make the offer. "Sure."

He stepped inside and she closed the door, though it was obvious she wasn't entirely comfortable doing so.

"If you prefer to leave the door open, feel free."

She looked up, blushed, her cheeks nearly matching her fiery red hair. "Am I that obvious?"

He smiled, forced a load of kindness he in no way felt into the expression. "Afraid so."

"I'll work on my presentation."

"I couldn't help noticing as I drove up, there's a couple of places on the roof that need some attention. You'll probably want to consider getting someone to do some caulking and painting around the windows and doors before winter, too. I've been doing a lot of that next door."

She nodded, her expression more worried than uncertain. "I can probably take care of those things myself."

"Maybe, but I can help if you'd like. I'm no expert but I'm reasonably handy."

She bit her lower lip for a second before she responded to his announcement. "I'm afraid this house has gone downhill since I saw it last. My brother— Levi—said he kept an eye on things but I'm not sure how much he would know about home maintenance.

And, to be honest, my grandmother always took care of things. She was a firecracker. I might have learned a lot more from her if I hadn't gone away." She stared at the floor a moment before meeting his gaze once more. "But I learn quickly. I can probably do most of it myself with some amount of instruction."

He nodded to the paint can and brush next to the front door. "Looks like you already have a start on things."

She tried to smile but didn't manage the feat. "Yeah. Some things can't wait."

She had painted over the unpleasant reminder of what she was labeled by some, but the vicious word still showed through her efforts.

"Is there anything I can help you with before I go?" He didn't want to overstay his welcome or push too far today. Slow, steady progress was the best plan.

She moistened the lip she had been chewing. "Well, I did notice that the stove won't turn on." She hitched a thumb behind her. "I was going to heat some water for coffee."

"I can have a look."

"That would be great. Thank you."

She led the way into the kitchen, not that he needed her to show him where it was. He had been through every inch of this house at least three times. She had a number of surprises waiting for her.

In the kitchen she gestured to the stove.

He turned a knob for a top burner, then the oven. Pretended to ponder the possibilities, then he said, "I should check your electrical panel."

She frowned. "The fuse box?"

He nodded. "If it was never upgraded to a breaker box then that would be it."

She shrugged. "I have no idea. My grandmother called it a fuse box."

"Let's have a look."

She guided him to what had once been a back porch but was later converted to a laundry room. A new, smaller back porch had been added. She gestured to the wall next to the door they had exited. "Right there."

The electrical panel in the house had been upgraded. Again, he took some time to look over the situation, then flipped a breaker—the one he had flipped to the off position a week ago. While he was at it, he took care of the one for the water heater, as well. That one, he supposed, had been turned off by whoever closed up the house after the grandmother passed away.

"I turned on the water heater, too." He tapped the breaker he meant. "If for some reason it doesn't work, flip it back to the off position and let me know. Let's see if that did the trick for the stove."

Back in the kitchen, he turned the knob that controlled the burner beneath the kettle and the light next to it flared red.

She smiled. "Thank you. I would not have made it through the morning tomorrow without coffee."

"If you need anything else, just let me know." He turned and strode back toward the front door. She followed. At the door he looked back to her. "Call if you hear or see anything that makes you feel uncomfortable. I'm a minute away."

"Thank you again." She frowned. "I don't mean to sound ungrateful, but why are you doing this?"

He searched her eyes, wondered what she would say if he told her the truth.

"I don't know what happened to you, but you seem like a person who needs a break."

He left before she could say more. No need to risk allowing her to see the truth in his eyes.

She watched from the door as he backed up and turned around. When he stopped at the road to see that it was clear, he glanced in his rearview mirror to find her still watching.

The lady was lonely and afraid. Good.

That was exactly the way he wanted her.

## Chapter Three

Cece prowled through the closet she had used as a teenager. She could not believe her grandmother had not thrown this stuff away. But then, her grandmother had been the only person who believed Cece was innocent and who hoped she would come back home one day.

*Home.*

She glanced around the room. This really was home. God knew she had spent most of her childhood here. After her mother died, her father had dumped her and her sister here more often than not. He had always dragged the boys along with him, as if they were more important than the girls.

Of course he had thought that way. Females were a lower life-form as far as he and his church creed were concerned.

*Church.* Cece felt certain it was wrong to call the following her father had created a church. It was a cult. One with harsh rules and absolutely no compassion. How had it survived nearly nine years without him? She could only assume Marcus had stepped fully into his shoes and used his murder as a platform for his own selfish purposes.

No surprise there. Marcus had always been cunning and self-absorbed. Sierra, too, for that matter. At least, once she passed the age of twelve. Cece and Levi had been the ones who were different. They were like their mother, her father had often accused as if it were a bad thing. All those times he had tossed Cece and her sister to their grandmother, poor Levi had been forced to go along with him and Marcus. She had heard her brother crying at night after many of their outings. When she had asked him what happened, he wouldn't talk about it. She could only imagine what Levi had suffered in the name of their father's twisted beliefs.

Levi still had not come to see if she made it home okay. She hoped nothing had happened to him. Maybe he had decided that staying on her side wasn't worth the trouble. If he had, she wouldn't blame him. Marcus and Sierra and their followers would make it especially hard on Levi for having any association with her.

Cece grabbed a nightshirt and panties from a drawer and made her way to the bathroom. She looked forward to the luxury of a long, hot soak.

She found a towel, soap and shampoo, and placed them on the edge of the tub. After setting the water to the hottest temperature she could bear, she stripped off the clothes some organization had donated to her since she had had nothing to wear when she left the prison. She spotted a couple of bruises from the stoning incident. She shuddered, tried to block the memory of another event like that one from long ago. She had

been around ten and the members of her father's following had decided one of their members had stolen
something from a fellow member. They had dragged
him outside the barn they had used for meetings back
then and thrown stones at him.

The man had eventually managed to run, escaping
their torture, but Cece had never seen him again. She
wondered if they had found him and finished him off.
She had no proof that her father or any one of his followers had ever killed anyone, but the hatred and evil
they spewed was so extreme, she couldn't help believing them capable.

She eased into the hot water and sighed. A bath had
never felt so good.

Until the water started to cool, she was content to
simply lie there and soak. Her muscles relaxed fully
for the first time in what felt like forever. Eventually
she washed the stench of prison from her hair and skin.
Even the soap and shampoos used in the prison carried
a distinct scent she would never forget.

When her skin felt raw from scrubbing, she pulled
the plug and climbed out. The towel was clean but
smelled a little stale from being folded up in the old
linen cabinet for so long. She would need to wash all
the linens, maybe hang them on the clothesline for air-
ing out. Probably be a good idea to do that with her
clothes, as well.

Dressed and feeling more comfortable than she had
in nearly a decade, she draped her towel across the
side of the tub and then marched out back to throw the

clothes she had worn out of the prison into the trash can. She never wanted to see or touch anything from that place ever again.

She made herself a sandwich and wandered into her grandmother's bedroom. Her hand slid over the pink chenille spread as she sat down on the side of the bed. Pink had been her grandmother's favorite color. Cece wished she had all the letters her grandmother had written to her over the years. Always on pink stationery tucked into a pink envelope. Two weeks after her grandmother passed away the letters had been taken from her prison cell and she never saw them again. No matter how many times she asked about them, she never received a straight answer.

Cece had finally given up.

Her grandmother had told her repeatedly in the letters that if, for some reason, she wasn't here when Cece came home, for her to be sure to go to their special place for a visit. She looked around the space, rested her gaze on the bookcase next to the window on the other side of the room. A fainting couch sat next to the bookcase. She and her grandmother would relax there for hours and read. When Cece had been too small, her grandmother had read to her. Later, they read their own books silently, but together. That reading nook was their special place.

Cece finished off her sandwich and walked over to the bookcase. She pulled out the well-worn copy of *Little Women*. The weight of the book and the beckoning scent of the pages made her smile. This had been one of their favorites. Cece had lost count of the number of times she'd read it.

Something slipped from between the pages and drifted to the floor.

She crouched down to feel for it beneath the edge of the couch.

Money.

A one-hundred-dollar bill.

"What in the world?"

Taking her time, she flipped through page after page in volume after volume. By the time she was finished, there was five thousand dollars stacked on the flowery sofa. What had her grandmother been thinking, leaving all that money in the house? She had a bank account. Mr. Frasier had said there was some amount of money in the account, but Cece would need to go to the bank and do the necessary paperwork to access it. She doubted there would be much but she genuinely appreciated whatever was there.

But why leave this cash here where anyone who wanted to break a window or bust open a door could stumble upon it?

Had her grandmother been afraid someone else would get their hands on the money in the bank account? Or was this her mad money? She had often spoken of her kitty. A little secret stipend she kept tucked away for emergencies, she'd always said.

Cece kept a couple hundred dollars in her hand but she climbed up on the chair and put the rest on top of the bookcase where no one would see it. Her grandmother had thought of everything, it seemed.

Her grandmother had been smart that way long before being prepared became a lifestyle of the slightly overzealous.

With no television to watch, she dug out the family photo albums and entertained herself with a walk down memory lane. Whenever she and her grandmother had looked at the albums, Emily always told the story behind each photo. Cece remembered most of them. There were lots of photos from the era before her mother died. Photos of Cece's grandparents with the whole family, even their father. But after her mother died, her father had drawn deeper and deeper into the cult that eventually became his own personal kingdom of followers.

He had pushed her mother's parents away and focused solely on the *church*.

Cece sneaked over to see her grandparents after school whenever she could. Marcus always told on her if he saw her. Levi and Sierra mostly did whatever Marcus said to do. But Cece had never conformed. She and her father had fought often—until he kicked her out at sixteen. The whole family had shunned her at that point. Eventually Levi had started to sneak opportunities to see her. Marcus and Sierra wanted nothing to do with her. Their father's approval was far too important.

She traced her fingers over a photo of her younger brother. Why had he not come to pick her up the way he promised?

Cece hoped he was okay. She had no way to call him—even though she now had a house phone. She didn't know what cell number he used or even if he owned one. He hadn't owned one when she was arrested. Her father had not allowed them to have cell phones. Cece had bought one after she moved in with her grandmother. She had no idea where it was now, not that it would still work since her contract had long since run out. Knowing her grandmother, if it had been given back to her, it would be here somewhere. The police may have kept it as part of their evidence. Images of being questioned, of all the blood, flickered one after the other through her head.

The memories were taking a toll on her emotions. "Enough for today."

She put the albums away and decided to tug on a pair of jeans and a tee and walk around the yard. It wasn't dark yet. Plenty of time for a leisurely stroll. She was relieved when the jeans she had worn at twenty still fit. She spotted a pair of flip-flops under the edge of the bed and pulled them on. The screen door whined as she pushed through it. The heat had finally started to ease a little as the sun brushed the treetops.

The yard was well maintained. She supposed the lawyer's office had someone cutting the grass. She had noticed the old lawn mower when she backed the truck out of the barn. If there was a gas can in there she would be in business. She could cut the grass when it needed it again. She had done it plenty of times when she lived here. Her grandmother had been old-school when it came to the distribution of chores. There were certain things that she considered man's work and cutting the grass was one of them. Cece had ignored her warnings about spending too much time out in the sun or making calluses on her hands and done most of the chores that had been her grandfather's.

On Monday she would need to get out there and look for a job and report in to her parole officer. As thankful as she was for the cash she had found, it wouldn't last forever. Though the house and the truck were paid for, there were insurance and property taxes, utility bills and food.

The idea that her driver's license was expired occurred to her. She would need to get that taken care of next week, as well. She did not want a ticket. Having an accident without insurance was not something she wanted to experience, either. If she wanted insurance, she had to possess a valid driver's license.

Crunching gravel echoed through the trees. Someone had turned into the driveway. Cece hurried into the house through the back door, locked it up tight and rushed to the front window to peek beyond the curtains to see who was arriving.

She didn't recognize the car. Older. Green. The driver's-side door opened and a man emerged. He turned toward the house.

*Levi.*

She grinned and hurried to the door, threw it open and rushed out to meet her little brother. He stared at her as she threw her arms around him. He seemed to have grown a foot since she saw him last month.

"I was beginning to think you had hit the road and didn't tell me," she said, squeezing him tighter. She was so glad to see him. "Especially after you didn't pick me up."

His body felt stiff beneath her touch. His arms were around her but weren't really hugging her. She drew back. "What's wrong, Levi?"

That was when she noticed his clothes. Plain, dark indigo jeans, plain white shirt. Work boots. Hair cropped short.

*He was one of them.*

"No." She shook her head. Searched his face, his eyes for some explanation.

He stared at the ground for a moment before meeting her gaze. "It was a long time coming."

*No. No. No.* "Levi, how many times have we talked about what they are? You can't be one of them!" Her entire body seized with the agony of it.

His hands braced against her arms, kept her at bay as if he could not bear to have her hug him again or get too close. "It was the right thing to do. Marcus and Sierra want me in the family."

She shook her head. "I don't care what Marcus and Sierra want. All that matters to me is what you want." She stared straight into his eyes. "Is this what *you* want?"

"It's what Daddy would want. What God wants."

Cece shook her head. She wanted to tell him that God had never been a part of this, but he knew without her having to lecture him. He knew all too well.

"I just wanted to make sure you made it home all right since I couldn't come pick you up." He dared to look at her then. "I love you, Cece. In time you'll understand this was the right thing to do."

Before she could argue, he turned and climbed back

into the car. She wanted to stop him, to argue with him, but she couldn't find the wherewithal to fight. If he had left town without telling her, run off to marry his latest girlfriend, gotten arrested for some small-time crime, she would have been far less devastated.

She watched him drive away and she understood with utter certainty that she had no one left.

No one. She was completely alone now.

Why bother staying in this damned place to prove her innocence? To find the truth?

What would it matter?

Who was left to care?

No one.

Cece wasn't sure how long she stood there but dusk had settled heavily by the time she made herself stop waiting for Levi to come back and tell her he'd changed his mind or that he had only been joking. She turned away from the empty driveway that was being overtaken by darkness and walked back to the house.

Inside it was dark enough to need the light on. She felt for the switch, flipped it up.

Nothing happened.

"For Pete's sake, what now?"

In the kitchen she found the flashlight her grandmother had kept in the tool drawer for as long as she could remember. She prayed the batteries weren't dead. She slid the switch and light gleamed across the room.

She breathed a sigh of relief and made her way to the laundry porch. She opened the door to the panel box and shone the light over the breakers. Everything looked to be as it should. Then why did she not have any lights?

Using the flashlight, she checked the lights in the other rooms. Nothing worked. Not the overhead lights, not the lamps.

She had no desire to be stuck out here all night with no electricity. The flashlight was handy but it was not the same thing as having a well-lit room. She went back to the kitchen and found the note with the stranger next door's name and number. Thankfully the telephone was connected through one of those regular old landlines and the phone was an ancient push-button, so it had its own source of electricity.

Two rings sounded before he answered. She took a breath and did what she had to do. "Mr. Ross, this is Cecelia Winters next door. I'm sorry to bother you but I have no lights. Nothing is coming on. I checked the panel box but I couldn't see the problem."

He assured her he would be right over. Cece thanked him and hung up the phone.

She pressed her forehead to the wall and hissed out a weary breath. She had been scarcely more than a kid when she went to prison. Growing up she had had chores and certainly she had helped her grandmother out when she lived here. But she had never been responsible for an entire house. She had no idea what things she needed to know, much less do.

Too bad they hadn't taught this kind of thing in prison. She could have used lessons for practical living.

However frustrating all this was, she reminded herself as she moved to the front window to watch for her neighbor, she greatly appreciated having a home to which to come. So many of the other women she had met in prison had nothing or no one waiting for them. Cece might not have any family left, but she had this small house and land. She had a little money.

She would manage.

If proving her innocence turned out to be impossible, she could always sell and get the hell out of Winchester.

Without Levi, there was nothing else keeping her here.

Headlights bobbed in the distance as a vehicle navigated the long driveway. She tightened her grip on the flashlight and hoped it was Mr. Ross. Being stuck here in the dark was less than reassuring. She should have already taken the time to find her grandmother's shotgun and the ammunition required to use it.

The driver's-side door of the truck opened and the interior light allowed her a glimpse of the man behind the wheel.

Deacon Ross.

Cece unlocked and opened the door. When he reached the porch, she offered, "I really am sorry to bother you again."

She felt confident the man had not expected to be taking care of a neighbor recently released from prison when he bought the Wilburn place. She kept the flashlight aimed at the floor to provide the necessary illumination without blinding either of them.

"No problem. You saved me from another bad episode of what used to be my favorite TV show."

He smiled and she relaxed. "I haven't watched much television in a while."

Prisoners were allowed some amount of television time but she had preferred to read. Reading allowed her to ignore the others. Maintaining a low profile had helped her to avoid trouble more than once.

"Trust me," he offered, "you haven't missed much."

She held out the flashlight. "You'll need this."

He took the flashlight, headed for the laundry porch and she followed. He was tall. Six-two or six-three, she estimated. Far taller than her five-three. Her lack of height was something else she had inherited from her mother and grandmother. Unlike her, her sister Sierra was dark haired and taller, more like their father. Marcus and Levi were the same. However much grief she had put up with as a kid being called "ginger" and "red," she was glad she wasn't like them.

The lights came on. "How did you do that?"

She wasn't sure how she would ever truly show her appreciation to this man.

"Have you been away from the house without locking the doors?"

She shook her head. "I took a bath. Took a walk around outside." She frowned. "And my brother Levi stopped by. I stood outside talking to him for a few minutes. Not long, though." The wary expression he wore unsettled her more than the question.

"Unless you have an electrical problem that's tripping the main breaker, someone came inside and flipped it to the off position."

She hugged her arms around herself. "Oh."

He turned off the flashlight and offered it to her. "Do you have a weapon, Miss Winters?"

"Cece," she corrected. "Call me Cece." She drew in an unsteady breath. "My grandmother had a shotgun. It's probably still in the house, but I'm not allowed to have a firearm."

She hadn't thought of that until this very moment. Legally, she could not possess a gun. She should have spoken to the sheriff about this when he stopped by. Now she felt like a total idiot.

"Let's not worry about the technicalities, considering you're out here all alone. I think you should keep it put away and don't mention having it until your rights to own a firearm are restored. If there's an emergency and you have to use it, a decent attorney could use the fact that it was actually your grandmother's and had been left in the house. You forgot about it. As simple as that."

It didn't sound simple to her but she didn't have any idea what else to do. "Okay."

"For now," he said, "let's make sure it's in good working order and loaded."

He was right. She should have done that already.

He followed her to her grandmother's room. Every light in the house was now on. The .410 was in the closet. A box of shells sat right next to it. She gestured in that direction. "She always kept it loaded."

Ross picked up the shotgun. He slid his thumb over the heart that had been carved into the stock.

"My grandfather carved the heart for my grandmother. He said this was the smallest shotgun he could get, making it manageable for her and yet still able to kick the butt of any trespassers."

"He was a smart man." Deacon racked the weapon and nodded. "Not much recoil. That click you heard was a round going into the chamber so it's loaded. We can take it outside and make sure it fires, if you want to be certain."

"Let's do that." At least she could protect herself if the need arose.

He led the way through the house and out the back door. Once in the yard, he took aim, not straight up but toward the treetops, and fired.

When the blast stopped reverberating in the air, he gave her a nod. "Fires and racks smoothly." He passed the shotgun back to her. "Keep one in the chamber and you won't have to waste time racking."

The rifle seemed to burn her hands and she couldn't wait to get back inside and put it away. "Thank you. I hope I won't have to bother you again."

"Like I said, call anytime."

She followed him back into the house. He hesitated at the back door. "Keep your doors locked, even when you're home and step out into the yard."

"Good idea."

At the front door she thanked him yet again and said good-night.

He studied her a long moment, then nodded and walked away.

She watched as he drove off and was grateful again for this stranger next door who had turned out to be a very good neighbor. She certainly hadn't expected sympathy or compassion or much else from anyone in this town.

With a shudder she quickly put the rifle away. She did not want any trouble, especially the kind that might get her sent back to prison.

What she understood with complete certainty was that the troubles she had experienced so far were only the beginning of whatever was coming. No one who had liked her father was going to be happy she was back. Most of them considered her vile…evil, something less than human.

There would be trouble. Her plan was to do what she had done in prison: keep her head down and search for the truth. It was the only thing left in this town that held any interest for her.

The hard part might just be staying alive long enough to find it.

## Chapter Four

Midnight was only minutes away when Deacon finally decided to call it a night. He had been watching her house for hours. She had turned out the lights an hour ago. As a precautionary measure, he had set up motion sensors at the edge of the woods around the house, several directed at the driveway. No one was getting close to her without his knowing about it.

Cecelia Winters had a lot of enemies in this town. Deacon did not want one or more of them getting in the way of his plan. He had wanted her to feel the pressure of coming home—the hatred, the shame—that was true. But no matter what she was guilty of, he did not want anyone hurting her physically. Even he wasn't that heartless.

He had waited a long time to find the truth about his missing partner; he wasn't going to allow some redneck with a grudge to screw that up now. Jack had a widow, he had two grown children who deserved to have closure.

Deacon had scarcely taken two steps along the path toward home when he heard the voices. They were too low to determine if they were male or female but there was definitely more than one. He eased into the copse of trees on the right to ensure his presence wasn't picked up in the moonlight.

The figures moved out of the woods, into the backyard. With the help of the light from the moon he recognized they were male. One carried what appeared to be a large black box. No, he decided, not a box. A gas can. Since they moved toward the barn, the two obviously planned to torch it.

Bad idea in more ways than one.

It had not rained in more than a week. The grass, shrubs and trees were dry. A setting for disaster. Frustration and impatience mounted inside him. These bastards likely didn't care the extent of the damage they caused, only that they wreaked havoc for the woman.

Deacon slipped along the edge of the woods bordering the yard until he reached the back side of the barn. The two were getting cocky now, talking a little louder, making more noise as they moved about to execute their dim-witted plan.

The smell of gasoline filled the air. One of the bastards had started to splash gasoline onto the barn.

Enough.

Deacon eased up behind the one with the gas can and pressed the muzzle of his weapon against the back of his head. "Don't move."

The man—the air—everything stilled for just a moment. A single moment that Deacon knew all too well. The fight-or-flight response would kick in next.

"If your friend lights a match I'm putting a bullet in your head," Deacon warned.

The guy dragged in a breath and screamed, "Mac!"

"You pull that trigger," the second man, the one named Mac, apparently, cautioned, "I'm pulling mine."

"Either way," Deacon pointed out with a nudge to gas man's head, "sucks to be you."

A shotgun blast exploded in the night.

The guy with the gas can dropped it and ran.

Deacon held the other man's gaze. The light from the moon glinted off the barrel of his weapon. "You still have time to run."

He held his position.

"Who's there?"

Cecelia's voice.

The sound of her racking the shotgun cracked the air.

Deacon's tension moved to the next level.

"I've already called the sheriff!" she warned.

Another second of locked gazes and the man, Mac, broke. He ran for the tree line.

Deacon let him. Better that than a shoot-out. The two were obviously amateurs. Likely paid or otherwise influenced to set the fire to terrify the owner.

"It's me!" Deacon called out as he tucked his weapon away and then stepped from the shadow of the barn where the moonlight would give her a clearer view of him.

She lowered the shotgun and turned on the porch light. "I heard voices."

"You had company." He walked toward the porch, scanning the tree line as he went. "We need a water hose."

While they rounded up a hose he explained about her late-night visitors and how he had heard the gunshot and come running. Not exactly the whole truth but as close as she needed to know. She was safe and the would-be troublemakers were gone for now.

Deacon used the water hose to dilute and wash away as much of the gasoline as possible. When he felt satisfied with the results, he put the hose away and followed her inside. She had dragged on jeans beneath the nightshirt. Her hair was a tangle of fiery curls. She still held onto the shotgun, but she had started to tremble. The adrenaline from the excitement was receding, leaving her shaken. Deacon took the rifle and put it away. Just in time, since two deputies arrived and took their statements, then had a look around. The abandoned gas can might provide fingerprints. The man who had been carrying it had not been wearing gloves. Just proved how cocky he was. He hadn't expected to get caught.

Deacon provided a detailed description of both men. He had not seen the vehicle in which they had arrived or departed. In fact, he had not heard one, either. Typically sound carried a fair distance in the dark, particularly in the country where there was little or no unnatural noise in the middle of the night. Obviously, they had parked a good distance away from their destination.

The deputies assured Cecelia they would do everything possible to identify the perpetrators. Deacon suspected that wouldn't happen unless the prints of the man carrying the gas can were in the system. He was betting they weren't, otherwise the guy wouldn't have been so careless. Men who had done time generally did not want to do more. Still, there was a chance. One or both may have been high or something, though Deacon didn't believe that to be the case.

When the deputies were gone, Cecelia stared at him for a long while before she mustered up the courage to say what was on her mind. "I still don't understand why you're doing all this."

He had been expecting that one. "We're neighbors. You want me to ignore the sound of a gunshot?"

She blinked, considered his explanation for a moment. "So you've decided that being my neighbor makes you my designated protector?"

She was angry now. This was a woman who wasn't accustomed to folks lending a hand to help. She was suspicious and rightly so.

"I guess I could tell you how my father raised me to be kind and helpful, particularly when a lady was involved."

Her expression warned that story was not going to cut it.

"When I bought the Wilburn place, I ran into your attorney, Frasier. He was here, checking on things. I stopped by to introduce myself to my new neighbor and he explained the situation. During the course of the conversation he asked me to keep an eye on you once you were released. I told him I would."

Her mask of skepticism slipped just a little. "He was a good man. He tried really hard to help me."

"I didn't know him that well, but I got the impression he was quite fond of you."

She relaxed visibly. "I think he was in love with my grandmother. I guess he felt compelled to see after me because of her."

"I know a little about your story," he said, choosing his words with care. "A lot of people appear to be angry with you."

Her arms hugged more tightly around her slim body. "I have no control over what people choose to think of me or how they decide to act on those thoughts."

"Do they have reason to be angry with you?"

Her chin came up in defiance. "Apparently they believe so."

"You didn't answer the question."

"I need a drink."

Surprised, he turned and followed her into the kitchen. She reached under the kitchen sink and retrieved a bottle of bourbon. He had noticed it there the first time he came inside and had a look around. He figured her grandmother kept it around for therapeutic purposes.

She poured shots into two glasses and handed one to him. "Thank you."

He accepted the glass. "No thanks necessary."

With one swallow she downed the shot, grimaced, then set her glass on the counter. "No matter that the thought crossed my mind on far more occasions than I care to name, I did not kill my father."

She exhaled a big breath, as if saying the words out loud somehow released a massive weight she had been carrying for entirely too long.

He downed his drink, wished for another but set his glass aside, instead. "You took the fall for someone else."

She leaned against the counter next to the sink. "I guess so. Not that I chose to or that I have any idea who I did it for. Don't get me wrong, I was glad he was dead. For a little while, I didn't even care who killed him. I assumed that the law would prove I was innocent—since I was. But that's not how it worked out."

To his surprise she reached for the bottle again and poured herself another shot. She offered the bottle to him but he declined. It was highly unlikely she had drunk anything that contained alcohol in more than eight years; one of them needed to remain stone-cold sober.

"So, you waited." He leaned against the counter on the other side of the sink.

"But the police claimed that all the evidence pointed to me. I was always the black sheep of the family so I wasn't surprised when Marcus and Sierra came out against me. Levi was the only one who stood by me."

"Was there hard evidence or was it mostly circumstantial?" He knew the answer but he wanted to hear what she had to say on the matter. His knowing too much would only make her more suspicious.

"Those last couple of months before his murder we had several public disputes. During at least one of those occasions I said I wished he was dead. It was the truth. I did. I hated him. Hated him for making my mother so miserable. Hated that she was dead and he was still alive. Hated what he did to our family—turning us against each other." She shrugged. "Basically, I hated him, period."

"That's hearsay—the arguments, I mean. There had to be other evidence."

"He called. Said he needed to see me. My grandmother warned me not to go. She said he would just try and talk me into coming back into the family." She turned, braced her hands on the counter and stared into the darkness beyond the kitchen window. "I should have listened to her. She had told me the stories of the things he said and did to my mother."

A moment of silence passed with her lost in her memories. To prompt her, he asked, "Why didn't you?"

"I guess all the way until the bitter end some part of me hoped to see a different side of him. Levi was having a hard time with all of it. He despised our father but he needed him. He was really young and he needed that male role model." She shook her head. "Not that our father was the proper kind, but some part of Levi still loved him anyway. So I went. Thought maybe he might be reasonable."

"Someone got there before you."

She nodded. "When I arrived, he was dying. He had been stabbed more than a dozen times." She drew in a big breath. "I think the autopsy report said nineteen."

Deacon had seen the photos from the crime scene.

It had been a bloody mess. Dozens of people had trampled the scene even before the law arrived, including Cecelia's older brother and numerous other followers from the church.

"No matter that I hated him, I tried to help. I tried to stop the bleeding. Tried to give him CPR when he stopped breathing."

She lapsed into silence once more.

"He didn't say anything to you?"

"He did, actually. Well, I don't know if he was speaking to me or just mumbling in general."

"What did he say?" The answer to that question was also in the case file.

That answer was the one thing in all of this that gave Deacon pause. Winters had been dead when the police and the others arrived. No one would have known what he said to her if she had not given that information in her statement. He wondered if she had regretted doing so.

"He said the same thing over and over." She turned to face him, met his gaze. "*You*. He kept saying *you*. It was like he had something to tell me or to accuse me of, but he couldn't get the rest of the words out."

"You had no idea what he might have wanted to tell you?"

She shook her head. "We weren't exactly on speaking terms. Mr. Frasier said he may not have meant anything. He was dying. It may have simply been the only word he could say, or he may have been disoriented and confused. He may not have been speaking to me. It's possible he didn't even realize it was me trying to help him."

"Who—other than you—had reason to want him dead?"

"That's the strange part." She closed her eyes a moment as if the bourbon had started to do its work. "His followers worshipped him. There were people in the community who disagreed with his religious beliefs, but as far as I know he had no enemies. Nothing was taken from the house. Someone walked in, stabbed him over and over and then walked out again."

"I'm sure the authorities at the time explained to you that the sort of murder you described was an act of passion. There was a great deal of emotion involved. The killer would have been in a frenzy. Not thinking clearly."

She appeared to consider what he said for a few moments. "I don't remember any one mentioning anything like that."

Deacon ignored the thought that crossed his mind. "When you walked in and found him, did you see any footprints in the blood around his body? A killer who goes off the deep end and commits a frantic act usually isn't thinking of anything else—like avoiding leaving evidence."

She rubbed at her eyes with both hands and then ran her fingers through all those curls. Her face was clean, like a child's. No residue of makeup, not even leftover mascara. Fingernails were trimmed short and unpolished. She looked fresh and innocent. The woman standing before him didn't fit the image he had envisioned all this time.

"I didn't notice footprints. When I was being questioned, one of the deputies mentioned that there was no indication of a struggle. Nothing overturned. Nothing broken. He was just lying on the living room floor with blood all over him."

"No one found this strange?" The idea annoyed Deacon far more than it should have.

"If they did, no one said as much to me. Mr. Frasier said they believed I walked in with the knife hidden under my sweater and that my first blow was the one that put him down. He didn't struggle because he couldn't."

He saw her hands tremble before she crossed her arms over her chest, tucking them away from view.

"They found no prints," she went on. "No nothing that pointed to anyone other than me."

"Frasier seemed to believe the police didn't pursue a real investigation," he said, "because they already had their killer."

"That's exactly what they did." She met his gaze again, determination in her own. "I'm not saying they didn't do anything, but it wasn't enough."

"Cops are only human," he reminded her.

She frowned, as if she had only just thought of something she should have recalled already. "Did you know Mr. Frasier?"

He hesitated, for a moment considered not telling her. "I spoke to him a few times."

Realization dawned in her eyes. "Are you the private investigator he hired?"

That had been his first lie when he arrived in Winchester. He had made it a point to run into Frasier. Had told him he was interested in the Winters case.

He had used the cover that he was a former FBI agent who had started his own PI firm and that he was interested in the case.

"I am."

"Why didn't you tell me?"

"Mr. Frasier died. That was the end of the investigation."

"Did the two of you find anything? Discuss anything or come to any conclusions I haven't heard about?"

She was annoyed that he hadn't told her this already.

"We didn't. What we did was talk over the case and how it was investigated eight years ago."

"You asked me all those questions to see what I would say." The statement was an obvious accusation.

"I did. Old habits die hard."

"You've already decided there's nothing I can do to find the truth."

Another accusation. "There's a lot you can do, Cecclia. The question is whether it will change anything."

In his opinion, it would not.

"I did not kill him."

As much as he didn't want to, he believed her. "Give me full access and I'll see if I can help you find the truth."

"What do you mean, full access?"

"Full access to you, to the case files."

"You haven't seen the files?"

"I haven't seen the files through your eyes."

She thought for a moment, the pulse at the base of her throat fluttering wildly. "All right. Where do we start?"

"Right now, we start with sleep. You've had a big day. I'll be over in the morning and we'll talk. See where we go from there."

"Okay."

"Good night, then. See you in the morning."

He had almost made it to the back door when her voice stopped him.

"Thank you."

He glanced back, studied the image of the woman who looked so alone, so worried and so damned innocent.

She could not be that innocent.

# Chapter Five

Twenty-four hours.

She had barely been home twenty-four hours and already people had thrown rocks at her and tried to burn down her barn.

"You're wasting your time, Cece," she muttered to herself.

She clutched her coffee cup more tightly and turned away from the window over the sink. All those years she had spent in prison she had told herself over and over that it didn't matter what people thought. That she did not care if no one believed she was innocent. She couldn't care less what these people thought of her.

But it was a lie.

She had been lying to herself. The people in this town had known Cece her entire life. Certain teachers she remembered from school had made her feel smart and relevant. A couple had urged her to go on to college but she had known that could not happen. There was never enough money or opportunity. Still, deep down she did not want those teachers to believe she had murdered another human—even one like her father.

In the living room, she stared at her reflection in the mirror next to the front door. She looked older than her twenty-eight years. Tired. Weary of this life and she had barely begun to live it. What did a man like Deacon Ross see when he looked at her? A woman? Or a screwed-up kid who had nothing but this old house and the spot of land it perched on?

She blinked away the thought. He was a kind neighbor, a man who had made a promise to her grandmother's lawyer friend to watch after her. Probably he saw her as an obligation—one he likely regretted having accepted.

"Don't even start, Cece."

She turned away from the mirror and walked across the room to the corner where the desk that her grandmother had used for letter writing stood. Until the day she died, her grandmother had clung to the handwritten form of communication. She had insisted that cell phones and the internet would be the end of polite society.

Cece found a notepad and pen. No matter that a mere twenty-four hours had passed, she understood one thing with utter certainty: she needed a project besides the search for the truth. Her grandmother had entrusted her with this home—the home she had worked hard to keep all those years as a widow. Whether Cece stayed or left, she owed it to her grandmother to take care of the place. Anything she did to shape up the house would be an investment for later if and when she sold it.

The mere thought was like a betrayal of her grandmother. But Cece knew Emily would understand whatever she decided to do. She had told her so in letter after letter. Her grandmother had not expected her to stay in Winchester.

"Paint." Cece wrote the word, shifting her attention to the necessary.

Next she jotted down roof, exterior caulk and paint. Deacon had mentioned those things. He had also offered to help. She would do as much as she could herself before she went to anyone else. As a kid she remembered her father's church going to the homes of the elderly and doing things like painting and general maintenance. Funny, no one had come to do any of those things for her grandmother.

"No surprise," she muttered. The people who belonged to her father's so-called church weren't good people.

They were followers of his hatred and cruelty.

No matter that she did not kill him, she was glad he was dead. Grateful not to have to wake up with the worry of running into him or having him show up unannounced to torture her with his hateful words.

She opened the front door to step outside and survey the roof and siding as best she could. A van rolling to a stop in the driveway caused her to stall on the porch. Her heart had already started to pound by the time her eyes and brain assimilated the name of the delivery service printed on the side.

"Morning." The man in the uniform waved as he walked around to the rear of the van. He opened the doors at the back.

Cece walked to the edge of the porch and started down the steps. "Morning."

Who would be sending anything to her?

The man rolled a hand truck toward where she stood. Three boxes were stacked one on top of the other.

"Cecelia Winters?" he asked as he stopped at the bottom of the steps.

"Yes." She looked from the boxes to him.

"These are for you." He passed her a clipboard. "Just sign at the bottom."

She stared at the form. "Who sent the boxes?"

"Clarence Frasier."

Cece's gaze connected with his. "That's impossible. Mr. Frasier died two months ago."

The man shrugged. "You would have to call the office to get the details. They'll be open on Monday."

She nodded. Told herself it was possible his office had sent them rather than have her come by to pick them up. She signed the form and handed the clipboard back to the waiting man.

"Thank you."

He looked from her to the boxes. "Look, we're not supposed to go inside, but I can pull these up the steps and right inside the door, if you'd like."

She nodded. "I would appreciate it."

"No problem." He smiled, and the expression sparked in his eyes.

He did not know her, of that she was confident. If he did, he wouldn't have smiled so kindly or even have made the offer to go beyond what was required of him.

He pulled the load of boxes up the steps, rolled the hand truck across the porch and through the door—just across the threshold, as he had said. He scooted the load off the hand truck and was out the door and down the steps with the efficiency of someone who had been doing the job for a good long while.

"Have a nice day!" he called as he headed back to his van.

Cece watched him load up and go. She waited until he had turned onto the road before going inside and closing the door. On second thought, she locked it, as well. Deacon had warned her to keep her door locked at all times. Considering last night's visitors, she intended to keep the doors and the windows locked. Thank God for the air conditioning window unit and the ceiling fans, otherwise she would be burning up.

A few minutes were required to find something to cut the tape on the boxes. She slid the knife blade along the edges until the flaps opened. Inside each box was another box, the sort in which files were kept. She stacked one after the other next to the couch. Then she removed the lids. An envelope with her name on it sat on top of the folders inside one of the boxes.

She opened the unsealed envelope. It was a handwritten letter from Mr. Frasier.

Cecelia,
If someone besides me has delivered these boxes, then I am dead. I don't expect that my death was any sort of unusual event. Probably a heart attack. My doctor has been after me about my blood

pressure for ages. I suppose I should have listened better.

First, your grandmother has left you a sizable savings at First Union. Last I checked it was fifty thousand and some change. She said you should buy something better than that damned old truck. You know she always hated the thing.

Cece gasped. Tears crowded into her eyes as she thought of the woman who had been more of a parent to her than the man who had boasted the title *father*.

Use it wisely. Since the house is paid for, this should tide you over for a bit. In addition, your grandmother left a scholarship fund for you to use for college. These funds cannot be used for any other purpose. She was quite sneaky about that. She knew how smart you are and she wanted you to have the opportunity to explore all possibilities. Don't let her down.

Lastly, these are my working files from your case. I only wanted you to have them so that you would understand the insurmountable odds that were stacked against you. You have served your time. Don't waste any more on this case. Move forward, put the past behind you. Proving your innocence will not give you those years back.

Your grandmother's greatest wish was for you to be happy. Grant her that wish, Cece. And yourself.

Sincerely,

Clarence Frasier

Cece swiped at the tears dampening her cheeks. College. She had not even considered college. Though she had taken a few random classes in prison, she felt too old for college. But she knew that wasn't true. Lots of people older than her went to college.

She drew in a shaky breath and placed the letter on the coffee table. She rubbed her palms against her jeans and reached for the first file in the first box. This one contained a copy of the arrest record along with her lovely mugshot.

God, she looked so young. She had been, barely nineteen. A kid. Flashes of memory detonated in her brain like tiny explosions. Her hands in her father's blood.

*You.*

He just kept saying that one word over and over.

And then nothing.

The police had arrived. Question after question was fired at her. Her father's closest followers had filed in, throwing around accusations, praying fervently, then accusing her some more. Marcus had shown up. He had ranted at her.

*What have you done?*

Then the handcuffs had gone onto her wrists. The deputy had recited her rights as they led her away from her father's house, his blood all over her.

She remembered being ushered into the back seat of the patrol car. The door closing with a thud of finality. The radio on the dash crackling with voices.

Codes and words she had not understood at the time but did now.

Homicide. Perpetrator. In custody. Numerous other

words and phrases that meant just two things: a man was dead, murdered, and they had the killer in custody.

End of story.

Except it wasn't true. It was a mistake. A setup. A lie.

Fury tightened her lips. She would go to college, just like her grandmother wanted. But first she had a story to rewrite.

Her story.

DEACON STARED AT the screen of his laptop. Cece sat on the sofa, file folders spread over the coffee table in front of her. She alternately cried and swore.

Part of him hated that he had planted cameras in her house and now watched her at a private moment like this. He kicked aside that too-human emotion. He needed the truth. Sympathy for her—this damned attraction he felt for her—would do nothing but get in his way. He had to remember those cold, hard facts. Ten years he had been in the Bureau. Ten years of training and hard work. His training had taught him not to get personally involved.

But that training had not been able to stop him.

He had spent months reading every single thing about this woman. Watching her at the prison. The warden had happily agreed to allow Deacon to stop by and observe the prisoner any time he wanted to. He had been allowed to read the incident reports, to interview her guards and other inmates.

He was well versed in most things that had happened to her inside those damned walls. Of course, not every incident was reported. The inmates had their own code. Cece had eventually learned to play by their rules. It was the only way to survive and she was a survivor.

One of the female guards he had paid to keep an eye on her had told him about the male guard who tried to rape Cece in the beginning. Another inmate had come to her aid in the nick of time. As it turned out, the Good Samaritan inmate was someone the attorney, Clarence Frasier, had paid to see after Cece. Well, he had not actually paid the inmate, he had taken care of the woman's mother and two kids for the service she provided.

Frasier had been that convinced of Cece's innocence.

That was the part that bugged Deacon. The reports and the scarce evidence backed his conclusions, but the lawyer and his passion about her innocence did not fit neatly into the scenario the former sheriff had built about Cecelia Winters.

The last part had not mattered to Deacon, not in all these months. And yet, in the past twenty-four hours, his confidence had started to slip. She had somehow breached his defenses, made him want to believe she was innocent. His training, his instincts, had kicked in the moment he first encountered her face-to-face. All those months of watching her from a distance, of reading the files—the same ones she read now—had not prepared him for the up-close encounter with her.

She exuded an honesty he could not deny and he hated himself for recognizing it.

He scrubbed a hand over his jaw and looked away as she set her face in her hands and started to sob.

Where was the evil, conniving woman he had expected? The one he had seen stand up to other inmates in prison? The one he had watched scrape her way through the final months of an eight-year sentence?

How had he seen that woman and not this one?

He closed his eyes as the answer echoed inside him.

She'd worn that tough mask to survive. He should have known—should have recognized the tactic—but he had not wanted to. He had wanted to see the heartless killer he had imagined her to be.

He had watched the taped interview of when she was questioned about his partner. She had sworn she did not know him. Had never seen him before. But she had lied. Deacon had recognized the lie in her eyes.

Whether she was responsible for Jack's disappearance or not, she knew something about what happened to him.

By God, he intended to find out what that something was.

He closed the laptop, grabbed his hat and walked out the door. He should stop himself right there, turn around and go back inside to watch her from a distance.

But that wouldn't get the job done.

He had to get closer.

Rather than walk, he drove to her house. During the short ninety-second trip he arrived at the perfect excuse for stopping by. It was easy. He had come up with dozens during the long planning stages of his strategy. All he had to do was pick one.

He parked, climbed the steps and knocked on her door.

She was slow to answer. Probably wiping away her tears and attempting to gather her composure. When she opened the door, it was clear she had failed miserably.

"Morning. I was headed into town for supplies and I thought you might want some more paint." He nodded to the door next to her. The red letters of the word *murderer* still lingered behind the layer of white she had brushed over them, giving the accusation a ghostly appearance.

He had spelled out that word with the red paint he bought at one of those hardware supercenters two towns over. He had wanted her to come home to that message, to feel the shame and the guilt.

He had watched Cece paint over the graffiti and he had hated himself for what he'd done.

Now, she stood in that doorway, her eyes red from crying yet again, and he hated himself even more.

Worse, he hated himself for hating himself.

How screwed up was that?

She moistened her lips, propped them into an unsteady smile. "Sure. That would be great. White exterior paint, please. I have money."

She turned and headed inside before he could stop her. She had found the money her grandmother had hidden for her.

There was more. He wasn't sure she knew about it yet.

He had interviewed her grandmother. The woman had believed Cece walked on water. Had adored her grandchild. He had pretended to want to help. That he had lied to the kind, elderly woman gnawed relentlessly at his gut even now.

He had done a lot of things over the past year he shouldn't have. Twice he had tried to forget. Had walked away and said he was done with the whole thing. Then a week or two later he was back, watching her again, asking more questions. Searching for that elusive truth he could not find.

He was a fool.

She was back at the door offering him a one hundred dollar bill. "I have no idea how much paint costs now. I need the stuff that blocks stains, too."

Her hand trembled ever so slightly as he stared at it. Before he could stop himself he closed his hand over hers. "What's happened that has you so upset?"

That his whole body yearned to hold more than her hand deepened that self-hatred rotting inside him.

"I received the files from my attorney's office. I've been going through them and…" She shook her head. "Sorry." She swiped at the fresh wave of tears that slipped down her cheeks. "I don't know why I'm so emotional. I haven't read anything I didn't already know about." She shrugged her slender shoulders. "But reading the statements—word for word—that recount the things my sister and older brother said about me was…painful. More so than I expected. It's ridiculous, I know. I sat in that courtroom and heard them answer the questions from the district attorney. But that was so many years ago and some of that time is like a blur. There was no shock or denial to soften the ugliness this time."

"People—even the people we think we know—can hurt us in ways we don't anticipate."

She stared up at him. Her eyes wide with sadness and uncertainty. "I tried to be a good daughter, a good sister, but I couldn't be what they wanted." She dropped her head, shook it. "Not even for Levi. I left. Left him and Sierra with that evil bastard and they were just kids."

His thumb slid over the inside of her wrist. "You were just a kid, too."

"A kid." She made a sound that was probably a stab at a laugh but did not quite hit the mark. "I was accused of murdering my own father before I was twenty. Left my baby sister and brother to fend for themselves when I was sixteen. I must have been a very bad person, Deacon. This kind of stuff doesn't happen to good people."

He released her hand before he turned any stupider than he already had. "How about a brush? You need a paintbrush? Drop cloth? Anything else?"

She shoved the money at him again. "Guess so."

He held up a hand and backed away a step. "I got this."

Turning his back, he had almost made it to the steps when she stopped him with a question he could not ignore.

"Why are you really doing this, Deacon Ross? I know I've asked you already." She shook her head. "I guess I keep expecting a different answer. Some hidden motive I don't see coming."

If he had hated himself before, he genuinely despised himself now. He faced her once more, the depth of the porch between them. "You need someone to care." He shrugged, his gut twisting with the words he did not want to say but could not hold back. "Now lock your door. I'll be back soon."

When he climbed into his truck and started to back away, she still watched him.

He barreled out of her driveway and onto the road. Anger blasted through him. He had to find a way to get back on track.

He owed Jack better than this.

He didn't owe Cece Winters one damned thing.

## *Chapter Six*

By the time Deacon returned, Cece had pulled herself together. Her eyes weren't red anymore and she didn't feel like such a complete idiot. What she felt was mad as hell. The things her sister and her older brother had said about her in those damned statements were lies—most of them, anyway—just like their answers in that courtroom.

She paced back and forth, the crumpled statements in her hand. Deacon's knock on the door reminded her that she needed to calm down. Sure she had the tears under control, but the anger was a whole new level of emotion. Her entire life she could not remember ever being this outraged. Not even when the jury found her guilty of murder. Those people had not known her. They had based their judgment on the evidence, which was completely against her, and an endless string of witnesses who had either embellished some semblance of the truth or flat-out lied.

Not even, she told herself, when the two deputies and the sheriff had treated her like a murderer. She'd had her father's blood all over her. The knife had been lying on the floor at her feet and though her prints weren't found on it, the district attorney suggested she had wiped away the prints.

This, she tightened her fingers on the wad of papers, was her kin. They knew her. Grew up in the same house with her. And they had lied.

Another knock echoed and she stopped pacing, drew in a big breath, let it out and strode to the door. Her fingers on the knob, she hesitated, reminded herself to make sure who was on the other side before she opened it. Just because she was expecting Deacon didn't mean it was him.

The man on the other side gave her a little wave and she told herself to relax. That did not happen. Her heart fluttered and she lost her breath all over again. She really, really was an idiot. This man was only being nice. The last time she had been touched by the opposite sex, the guy had been a boy—not a man—and that had been a very long time ago. And he was a jerk. She had been way too naive.

She forced her gaze down to the bucket in his hand. "Thanks."

"Looks like you've been working."

She followed his gaze to the coffee table and couch. Documents were spread all over the place. "Yeah. I've been…working."

"Why don't you get back to it and I'll take care of the door. This paint has a built-in stain blocker. A couple of coats should do it. When you're ready, you can walk me through what you have."

He smiled that smile that did not mean anything, yet her pulse still reacted.

She nodded. "Sure. That would be great."

Taking another deep breath, she returned to her piles. She knelt between the coffee table and couch, settled the wadded statements there and attempted to smooth them out. She shouldn't have reacted so angrily. She wasn't a kid anymore. She needed to handle all these emotions like an adult.

On some level she still felt like that nineteen-year-old who hadn't experienced the world. She had lived in Winchester her entire life. Never been farther than Nashville to the north or Birmingham to the south. She had never even seen the ocean. Navigating all this— she stared at the mass of papers—was difficult. She smoothed at the pages some more. Didn't help.

"As long as you can still read them, that's all that matters."

Her attention shifted to the man who'd propped open her front door and placed a drop cloth on the floor beneath it. His hand wrapped around the handle of the brush and her gaze followed the long brush strokes. His method for applying the paint was not at all like the smear process she had used.

"I guess I didn't like what I read," she confessed.

"You want to start with that?"

He was a stranger. He didn't know her family beyond their fanatical religious affiliations. She supposed he could be a good sounding board. Objective. She could definitely use an objective opinion. And he was a private investigator. He was an experienced investigator. Frasier had trusted him. She should, as well.

"When I was arrested, the police interviewed a lot of people who knew me and my father." She sat back on her heels and let her mind drift back to that dark time. "The reviews were mixed. Most folks lumped the whole Winters clan into the same category of fanatical misfits."

"Human nature." He glanced at her. "People see what they expect to see. What they want to see."

She bit back the question on the tip of her tongue. She wanted to know what he saw. "I didn't hold it against them. Still don't. Like you said, they see what they expect to see. I guess I hadn't given anyone a reason to see anything different."

"You were a kid."

She nodded. "True."

Cece wondered how old he was. Maybe thirty-two or thirty-three. Smart. Probably went to college. Most likely had a nice family.

She did not have a nice family. Since they had all turned their backs on her, she didn't really have a family at all.

"My older brother…" Saying his name was like a knife to her chest. She wondered if any amount of time would make that hurt go away. "Marcus, he stated that I was unbalanced and angry. That I'd said I hated our father on numerous occasions."

"He lied."

Was that doubt she saw in his eyes. After all, surely

one's own brother wouldn't say such things. "About most of it, yes," she clarified.

"Which parts did he lie about?"

He did not look at her this time, just kept painting. She expected any moment that he would start looking at her the way everyone else in town did. It was highly likely that she wouldn't be seeing as much of this new neighbor after today. But then he'd been over the case file with Frasier. She wasn't telling him anything he didn't already know.

"I've never been unbalanced in my life."

When he looked at her with surprise she had to laugh. "Like you said, I was a kid. I probably told the bastard that I hated him a hundred times. I did hate him. And I was angry, very angry. I hated what he had done to our family, particularly our mother. I hated everything about him." She sighed and then said the rest. "I had probably wished him dead a thousand times, maybe more."

"But your brother didn't know that part?"

Cece shook her head. "I'm sure he knew but he chose to use that information in a way that suited him. What Marcus said didn't surprise me. He and I weren't that close. It was Sierra who threw me under the bus. We were really close growing up. I told her how I felt. Usually when I was so angry I couldn't stop myself. She gushed the mean things I had said to the jury so tearfully, they were certain the words were tearing her apart. But that wasn't the case at all. I could see it in her eyes. She was enjoying the attention and she loved making me look bad. Even though I was the one who had helped her out too many times to count."

"You think someone was directing her? Maybe your older brother?"

"Possibly." Marcus had wanted Cece out of the picture permanently. "He knew there were people in the church who would listen to me if I decided to speak out against him."

"You never spoke out against your father?"

She shook her head. "My grandmother was afraid if I did that something bad would happen to me. The way it did to my mother."

Cece stared at the crime scene photos of her father lying in all that blood. Her shoe prints in the mess. Blood all over her hands, her clothes. No matter that she had hated him—despised him for all those years—as he lay dying and unable to be cruel or hurtful, she'd felt pain. The little girl in her who had loved the man who was her father had felt fear, anguish, shock at seeing him in that condition. Her most basic instinct had been to help him. To cry out for assistance.

"What happened to your mother?"

Cece's attention snapped back to the present. "I'm sorry, what?"

"You said your grandmother mentioned something bad happened to your mother."

She frowned. Why in the world would she tell this stranger all these terrible things about her past? If Frasier hadn't told him that part, maybe she shouldn't. Even as the thought entered her mind, memories from more than two decades ago rushed into her head.

Voices and sounds from that night. She had only been six. Her sister had just turned two; Levi was four. Marcus had been twelve. The screaming woke her. Cece remembered getting up but Marcus was there, in the darkness. He had ushered her back to bed. Sierra clung to her, crying. Levi was hiding in the closet. It wasn't until the abrupt silence that Cece realized the screaming had been coming from her grandmother.

The sun came up on the next day before she understood what had happened. Her mother had fallen down the stairs. Her father had tried to help her but could not. Her grandmother had arrived in the middle of it all. Cece did not really understand that part but her grandmother would never talk about it. She just said something terrible had happened and she did not want anything like that to happen to Cece.

"My grandmother believed my father killed my mother. I'm certain of it." Cece had never said those words to anyone else. Not even Levi.

Deacon asked her to start at the beginning, the morning before that night. It took a while for her to pull all the memories from the place to which she had banished them. Slowly, she pieced all the parts together. By the time she finished he had put his paintbrush down and joined her on the floor between the couch and coffee table.

"Did you ever confront your father about your memories of that night?"

How could he seem to care so much? Had she been locked away for so long she couldn't tell the difference between basic human kindness and whatever else it was she believed she saw in his eyes?

What she *wanted* to see in his eyes?

"I did. One morning when I was sixteen and it was just the two of us, I blurted out that I thought he killed her. That's when he kicked me out. He said if my grandmother was going to fill my head with lies, I could just go live with her."

"But she never confirmed your belief?"

She shook her head. "No. But I saw the truth on her face. She was afraid of him. I'm sure he threatened her that night."

"What about your grandfather? Was he still alive then?"

"He was, but he was blind and confined to a wheelchair." She closed her eyes against the memory of her grandfather sobbing at her mother's funeral.

"You've been through a lot."

His words drew her back to the present. "Mine was not a pretty childhood."

"What about Levi? You didn't mention his statement to the police."

With him sitting so close she saw the lines at the corners of his eyes. He looked genuinely interested in knowing what happened. Was she so desperate for an ounce of human kindness that she would imagine his concern?

"Levi insisted I wasn't capable of murder. He believed it was Sierra. She was acting all weird about our father. Possessive and at the same time rebellious against his rules. He told the police as much in his statement. But it didn't change anything. Sierra had an alibi."

"Don't tell me," Deacon said. "Her alibi somehow involved Marcus."

"Her car had broken down and he went to her rescue. Sierra's boyfriend, who was a mechanic and a member of the church, helped, too."

"Convenient."

"Very."

They sat in silence for a long moment until he finally asked, "So, what's the plan?"

She laughed. "Who says I have a plan?"

"You were in prison for eight years. You had a lot of time to plan what comes next."

Relaxing against the couch, she decided maybe he did care. Not everyone in the world had a hidden agenda. Some people were genuinely good. "At first I mostly just concentrated on surviving. Eventually—when I was more confident that I might live through being there—I started to think about when I got out."

"And here you are." He smiled, glanced around the room. "Ready to find some answers."

"I thought about not coming back."

She had made up her mind to come back and stay with her grandmother until she passed away and then move on. But her grandmother had died before Cece was released so she didn't get the chance. Why bother coming back with her grandmother gone? It would have been so easy to just never return. To forget this place. It should be even easier to leave now that Levi had abandoned her, too.

But life had never been easy for Cece and the trouble in the walking-away scenario was the idea that her grandmother had still been trying to prove Cece was innocent when she died. That reality changed something deep inside her. Cece needed to finish what her grandmother had started.

When she had finished relaying all this to her neighbor, he said, "Revenge is a very strong motivator."

If he only knew. "I guess so."

More of that silence settled between them.

She should probably say something but the quiet felt too comfortable to interrupt. Not at all like the noisy environment at the prison. So noisy and yet she had felt utterly isolated. Alone. There had always been the fear that the other shoe was about to drop…that something bad would happen at any second. Most of the time it did.

"I'll clean up that brush and have a look at the roof before I go. If you need anything, I can pick it up next time I'm in town."

"Sounds great. If you're sure you want to be that neighborly."

He got to his feet. "I'm sure."

Cece scrambled up and followed him to the door. "I have money. I can pay you."

He stared at her for a long moment. She couldn't quite label what she saw in his eyes, but it made her wish she had not said anything.

"I don't want your money." He reached for the brush and the bucket of paint.

She really was out of practice with how to read and

to communicate with everyday people. "Okay. Sorry. I didn't mean to offend you."

When he met her gaze again, the strange look was gone. "It's all right, really."

But the tension she sensed in him told her it wasn't all right. That moment was the first time she had felt uncomfortable in his presence. It was as if the neighborly stranger had suddenly disappeared.

Had she made another mistake trusting this man?

JUST BEFORE MIDNIGHT one of the many alarms he'd put in place went off. Deacon straightened away from the files he had been reviewing. Checked the monitor and didn't see anyone outside the house. Cece had gone to bed. He grabbed his handgun, tucked it into his waistband and headed out. Could be an animal, but he preferred not to take the chance, particularly after last night.

He knew the path between their properties so well he didn't need a flashlight. A thin sliver of moonlight managed to cut between the trees every few yards, enough to ensure he didn't veer from the path. By the time he reached the tree line the sound of engines was loud in the air.

One was a four-wheel-drive truck, the sort with lifts that caused it to sit chest-high off the ground. The other was an SUV. Both dark green or black. Both blasting music and filled with drunk or just plain rowdy scumbags.

His cell vibrated in his pocket. It was her. He answered with, "I'm here. Call 911."

This wasn't going to be like the jerks last night. Those two had been sober and fully capable of being scared.

The ruckus these guys were causing just climbing out of their vehicles warned that the bastards wouldn't be scared of much. Not in their condition.

Never a good thing.

If Deacon could get the drop on one, he would gain the upper hand. He moved through the shadowed tree line. Counted heads as he went. Four. All sounded drunk or high and ready to cause trouble.

"Come on out here, Cece Winters!" The one who appeared to be the leader shouted.

He stood at the bottom of the porch steps.

The porch light flared to life and the front door swung open.

"Oh, hell," Deacon muttered.

She stepped out onto the porch, the shotgun in her hand aimed at the SOB at the bottom of the steps.

The commotion that followed sent Deacon's tension skyrocketing. Three weapons—looked like hunting rifles—suddenly appeared in the hands of the man's buddies, all aimed at Cece. Deacon palmed his gun.

Anything he did at this point could cause one of these drunken fools to pull the trigger.

"I called Sheriff Tanner," Cece warned. "He and his deputies are on the way right now."

"Good," one of the idiots said. "They'll get here just in time to pick up the pieces of your skinny ass from all over that porch."

The man at the bottom of the steps twisted around

to face his friends. "Show some respect. Put those damned guns away. Right now, damn it!"

"She's got a shotgun aimed at you!" one of the three said. "Hell, man, she killed her crazy daddy. What's to keep her from killing you?"

"Hell, I ain't afraid of Cece. We used to be sweethearts. Now put your guns down and get back in your damned vehicles while I talk to the lady."

So this was the one boyfriend she'd had before going up the river. Evidently he wasn't any smarter than he'd been all those years ago.

The three weren't too happy, and they let it be known, but they did as their leader instructed. All three climbed into their vehicles and turned the music even louder. If Deacon was lucky the sheriff would get here before things got too interesting.

Deacon moved back through the tree line until he was parallel with the porch. The best he could tell, the man wasn't armed, but he could be carrying a piece in his boot. No way to make a firm determination.

"I just came to talk to you, Cece," the man said. "You should have called me when you got home. I can't believe I had to hear it on the street."

She laughed but didn't lower her shotgun. "Ricky Olson. Now why in this world would I call you? You never came to court to see how my case was going even once. You never even wrote me a letter all those years I was in prison."

"You're right." He nodded, grabbed the handrail to steady himself. "I was a total jerk. I should have come to see you before it was too late. I should have written."

"What do you want, Ricky? Like I said, the sheriff is on the way."

He climbed a couple of steps. "I just want to talk."

Deacon braced to move.

"We have nothing to talk about. You're drunk, Ricky. You should go home."

To her credit, she held her aim steady.

He climbed the final two steps. "I need to show you how sorry I am." He pounded a fist against his chest. "I should have taken better care of you. What happened was partly my fault. Your daddy was a piece of garbage and I should have testified on your behalf. It was the least I could do. That lawyer of yours asked me to, but my folks didn't want me to get involved. We were kids. You know, we did what our folks told us." He shrugged. "Most of the time, anyway."

"Well, I appreciate your apology, Ricky, but that's all water under the bridge. I've moved on. You should, as well."

He walked right up to her, allowing the muzzle of her shotgun to bore into his chest. Deacon gritted his teeth. This was going to get ugly.

"I want to make it up to you, Cece, baby."

"Go on, Ricky," Cece warned.

The music in the vehicles abruptly went silent. Whatever was about to happen, the guys with this asshole were anticipating a move.

Deacon had one chance and this was it.

He bolted out of the clearing at a dead run and was on the porch next to Ricky whatever-the-hell-his-name-was before the other guys could react. The barrel of his Glock bored into the man's temple. "Back off, Ricky."

Doors opened and curses swarmed in the air.

"In the house," Deacon ordered Cece.

She hesitated. Her eyes round with fear.

"Now," Deacon roared.

He wrapped his forearm around Ricky's throat and whirled him around, using him as a shield from the others. He stabbed the muzzle a little harder into his temple. "Tell your friends to back off, Ricky, and we won't have a problem."

Rifles were aimed at Deacon's head. He split his focus between the three approaching the steps and the idiot backed against his chest.

"I guess we've got a problem," Deacon threatened as he gouged the barrel a little harder.

"Hold up." Ricky held out his hands to his friends. "Let me and this gentleman talk for a minute, boys. We seem to have a little misunderstanding."

The three stopped in their tracks.

"You better hurry up, Ricky," the tallest of his buddies reminded. "She said she called the sheriff."

"Go on now," Ricky urged. "Get in the truck. Let me handle this."

When the three did as he asked, he spoke again. "You put your weapon down and I'll be on my way. I didn't come here for trouble. I just came to see her."

Deacon lowered his weapon but he didn't tuck it away. "Don't come back, Ricky. She doesn't want to see you."

Deacon dropped his arm from the other man's throat.

And then the dumbass went stupid.

Rather than walk away, he twisted and socked Deacon in the jaw.

Cheers went up from inside the parked vehicles.

The guy got in another punch before Deacon could get his weapon tucked away, then he leveled old Ricky with one solid cross.

Two seconds of silence echoed from the vehicles before the doors flew open. The three sidekicks rushed forward, rifles aimed.

Deacon knew better than to reach for his own. Instead, he raised his hands in surrender.

The door behind him opened and Cece was suddenly standing in front of him, her shotgun aimed at the threesome.

"Back in the house, Cece," he ordered.

She ignored him. "Get the hell out of here," she shouted to the three and then she shoved Ricky down the steps with her foot. "And take this piece of trash with you."

Blue lights throbbed in the darkness. Two patrol cars skidded to a stop between the trespassers and the porch. Deacon took the weapon from Cece.

Tanner and his deputies cuffed and loaded up Olson and his friends. Tanner took Deacon's and Cece's statements and then assured her that wreckers would arrive shortly and haul the trespassing vehicles away.

Tanner studied Deacon a moment before he left. There would be questions from the sheriff. He was suspicious of Deacon. Smart man.

For the first time in all these years, Deacon wondered if he was any better than the scumbags the deputies just hauled away.

"You need some ice for that jaw."

Deacon turned from the window and faced her. "It's not that bad. A lucky swing."

She laughed. A real laugh. The sound startled him. Free and relaxed, sweet.

"It is that bad," she countered as she reached up and touched his jaw.

He flinched and drew away.

She dropped her hand, obviously confused by his reaction to her touch. "Sorry. Let me get some ice."

He watched her walk away. It was only at that moment that he realized she was wearing just the night-shirt. No wonder Tanner had eyed him so speculatively.

Damn.

When she returned with ice wrapped in a hand towel he hadn't moved from the spot where he was standing when she left him.

She offered it to him. "I really am sorry about all this. I shouldn't have called you."

He clenched his fingers in the towel lumpy with ice. "I hope you're not serious. I think you can likely imagine what would have happened during the twenty minutes or so it took Tanner and his deputies to arrive."

He exiled the images from his mind.

When she said nothing, he added, "Your old friend came here to hurt you."

She nodded. "I'm well aware of his intentions and I genuinely appreciate your help." Her arms went over her chest. "But this is not your problem. It's mine.

You've been a really good neighbor. Gone above and beyond the call. But it's not fair that my tragic life is doing all this…" she gestured to his face "…to you."

"Life isn't fair sometimes." He jammed the ice against his throbbing jaw.

She stared at the floor as if she wasn't sure what to say next. He understood perfectly the juncture where things had gone wrong. Damn it.

He reached out to her, touched her arm. She stared at his hand.

"I overreacted when you touched me. I'm sorry for that. I just don't want you to get the wrong impression."

She looked up at him. "That you want to take advantage of me somehow because I'm this helpless woman who's all alone?"

He hoped she didn't see the guilt in his eyes. He was the one dropping his hand away. "I—"

"First, I'm not helpless. Second, do you know how long it's been since someone who wasn't wearing a prison uniform touched me?"

The air in the room suddenly seemed too thick to draw into his lungs. "I'm a little unclear on what you might want me to say to that."

She shook her head. "I don't want you to say anything. I want you to touch me." She took a step closer. "I want you to kiss me. I want you to make me feel something besides anger and resentment."

He told himself not to touch her—to walk away. He couldn't do it. He reached out, cupped her cheek in his hand, slid his thumb over her bottom lip. His body tightened with need and he hated himself for it.

"One day you'll look back and be glad that I chose this moment to say good-night." He lowered his hand and turned away.

"Please don't go."

Despite his every effort to keep walking, he stopped. Cursed himself for the weakness.

"I don't want to be alone. I feel like I've been alone forever."

Somehow he found the strength to face her once more without grabbing her and kissing her into silence…and doing all the things that were suddenly rushing into his head. "I'll stay." He pointed to the sofa. "Right there and you'll be in your room."

She nodded. "Fair enough."

He felt guilty about that, too.

There was nothing remotely fair about his motives.

# Chapter Seven

*Sunday, August 4*

She was going to church.

It was Sunday, after all. She had as much right as anyone else to do so.

Cece checked her reflection in the mirror over the dresser. Her skin was way too pale to wear this sundress but she didn't care. Prison did that to a person. She wanted them to see what they had done to her with their lies.

Would it matter?

No. They wouldn't care.

She took a breath and turned away from the mirror. Whether it mattered to them or not—whether it made the slightest difference, she wanted all of them to know. She wanted them to hear what she had to say.

*They* being her older brother and her sister.

Maybe she should include Levi. After all, he was one of them now. What could have happened since she saw him last month? In all this time he had never mentioned going to the other side.

He'd always hated the church and their father's followers.

What could Marcus have on Levi that had suddenly caused such a turnaround?

Evidently enough to keep him away from her beyond that brief drive-by. Maybe Marcus had made some threat that backed Levi off. Her little brother had always yearned for his older brother's approval, even when it was wrong.

Eight plus years ago they had all had their say.

Today she intended to have hers. She opened her bedroom door and the smell of fresh-brewed coffee filled her lungs, reminding her that *he* was here.

Deacon Ross. Warmth spread through her despite the cold that lingered with thoughts of the family who had abandoned her. Just as quickly she went cold again. She had practically begged him to kiss her and do anything else he might want to do. She closed her eyes and shook her head. How would she ever look him in the eye again? He no doubt thought she was every bit as pathetic as the rumors suggested.

She opened her eyes and faced the facts. She was. Pathetic, that was. As embarrassing as it was to confess—even to herself—her one sexual experience had been with the jerk who showed up drunk on her porch last night. In fact, the only boy who had ever kissed her was that same knucklehead. Unless she counted the guard who had forced his mouth over hers and would have raped her if not for the interference of the one inmate in the whole prison who had cared enough to step in.

Such a sad, miserable life.

Her grandmother had left her a college fund and some money. She should just leave now and never look back.

But she couldn't. She owed it to her grandmother to do this. Besides, if she didn't, this would haunt her the rest of her life. Her education, any career she attempted, would all be impacted by her record as a convicted murderer—a killer.

She had told herself a million times that it didn't matter. She didn't care what anyone else thought. But that had been a lie. She wanted people to know the truth, especially the people in this town who had been so quick to condemn her. No one had cared enough to save four kids from a fanatical, no doubt insane father when their mother died. Everyone had just looked the other way and allowed him to drag them into his obsession.

Those same people had jumped at the chance to condemn her after his murder.

One way or another she was going to show them all. She was innocent.

For the first time since she'd realized that she was going to be released, she knew what she wanted.

She wanted them to know her grandmother had been right about her. She wanted her life back.

The one someone in this town had stolen from her.

With a renewed sense of determination, she went to the kitchen where Deacon leaned against the counter with a mug of steaming coffee in his hand. She stilled, thought of the way that hand had felt against her cheek.

"Good morning." He lifted his mug. "Coffee's hot and strong."

A glance at the clock told her she had slept until past eight. She could not remember when she had last done that. Of course, they had been up most of the night. She was glad to see his jaw wasn't swollen and the bruise was so small it was hardly noticeable.

"Good morning. Wait." She stared at the coffeepot on the counter. "I don't have a coffeepot."

"I went next door and got mine."

"Oh. Well, thanks." She crossed to the pot and poured herself a cup.

"I take it you have plans this morning." He nodded to the dress she wore.

She braced her hip against the cabinet and sipped the hot coffee, mostly to buy time. When she had savored the bold brew, she said, "I'm going to church."

He set his mug aside and leveled his gaze on her. "Unless you're going to First Baptist or over to the Methodist one, I would think long and hard about taking that step. I don't think anyone's going to welcome you with open arms."

She downed another swallow, scalding her throat. "It's a free country. I'm a free woman. I can go wherever I want."

He shrugged one broad shoulder. "That's true. If that's what you really want to do, I suppose there's nothing stopping you."

"Nothing at all."

She focused on the coffee until she had finished it.

He did the same. Rather than go for more, she rinsed out her cup and announced that she was ready to go.

"Would you like to come with me?" She had not actually planned to ask that, but there it was…hanging in the air between them.

"Do you want me to come with you?" Those brown eyes of his watched her steadily, assessing her motives.

He did a lot of that assessing. She didn't actually mind. She had lived with deceit for so long she very much preferred straightforward. Other than that one off moment, this man had been more straightforward with her than anyone she knew.

"I was thinking it might be a good idea in case I run into those guys from last night." She hadn't really thought about that at all, but it sounded as good as any other excuse that popped into her mind.

"I think maybe you're right." He rinsed his mug and sat it on the counter next to the sink. "What time does the service start?"

"Not until nine, but I want to speak to the *reverend* before the crowd arrives." Marcus was about as much a reverend as she was…as their father had been.

"I'll drive."

"Thanks." Relief filled her. She hadn't been looking forward to facing Marcus alone. But she would have done exactly that if necessary. She wasn't going to permit fear to paralyze her.

She locked the door, checked to ensure the lock engaged. Deacon waited for her at the steps. They walked to his truck together. He opened the door for her and she climbed into the passenger seat. He closed the door and walked around the hood. It occurred to her that she really knew very little about this man. He was her neighbor. Relatively new in town. That first day, in the parking lot at Ollie's, the police officer seemed to know him. Surely that was a good sign.

Hadn't she already decided she could trust him?

When he slid behind the wheel, she asked, "Where did you live before you bought the Wilburn place?"

He started the engine, his gaze locked on hers. "A few places. Nashville, Louisville, and a couple of years in Mobile. But most of my time has been spent in Nashville."

"Where did you go to school?"

He checked the road in both directions before pulling out of her driveway. "UT."

The University of Tennessee. She was impressed. "What was your major?"

He glanced at her before refocusing his attention on the road. "You nervous or did you suddenly decide you needed to know me better?"

Her cheeks flushed. "Both, I guess. I woke up this morning and realized I don't really know very much about you. What I do know is good, but…" She shrugged. "You know."

"I do. What else would you like me to tell you?"

"What do you do? Besides rescue needy neighbors, I mean."

He flashed her a smile. "I'm an employee of the federal government but I'm currently on leave. I'm considering a career change. Maybe I'll go into the private sector and stick with private investigations."

*Federal government* could mean any number of things. She supposed he didn't want to talk about it and she certainly had no right to demand an explanation.

"I thought maybe you were already a private detective." He'd said he'd helped Frasier with her case, hadn't he? She had thought his being a private investigator and working for her attorney explained his dedication to helping her out of all those tight spots she'd found herself in since her release.

"Only on occasion."

Before she could ask anything else, he made the turn onto the road that ended in a graveled parking area surrounding an old-fashioned church. It was only about twenty-five years old but it had been built to look as if it were an original structure from the town's settlement. Inside was nothing more than a huge room of worship and two bathrooms that were tucked behind the stage-like pulpit. Between the bathroom doors were the stairs to the basement.

The white building with its plain, handmade wooden cross looked exactly the same as it had when she exited those doors for the last time nearly twelve years ago. She had walked out on one of her father's sermons when she was sixteen and she had not set foot back inside those doors since. Two entwined S's stood above the double entrance doors.

Salvation Survivalists.

*Walking God's path of readiness.*

All of it was based on lies.

"Do you know if he's here?"

Cece pushed aside the troubling thoughts and studied the SUV parked to one side of the building. The emergency exit was on that side. Her father had always parked there, choosing to enter by the side door rather than the front. But when it was time for his followers to arrive, he would be found standing on that stoop, front and center, with the double doors open wide.

Cece's stomach cramped. How she had hated the man. No matter that he was her biological father, he had been a devil.

She shook her head. "That SUV is parked where my father always parked so I'm assuming that's Marcus." She reached for the door handle. "I'll know soon enough."

Deacon put his hand on her arm, waylaying her. "I can go in with you."

She shook her head. "He won't say what's really on his mind in front of anyone but me. A good liar never reveals his true self in front of anyone he can't discredit or control."

At least that's the way it had been when they were kids. She stared at the building that should be the setting of a horror flick. They weren't kids anymore. She had not laid eyes on Marcus or Sierra since the day she was pronounced guilty, more than eight years ago. To some degree she could almost understand what made Marcus do the things he did—he wanted to be like their father. He wanted all that their father had built. Sierra was a different story. When they were little, he'd treated Sierra no differently than he had Cece. By the time she was a teenager, she could do no wrong. He'd treated her like a little princess.

"I'll be standing outside the truck. Scream if you need me."

She shook her head, could not stop the smile. "Will do."

The gravel crunched under her sandaled feet as she slid out of the truck and closed the door. She was truly grateful her grandmother had kept all her stuff. She hadn't had much but she was thankful for it now.

She stared at the closed double doors a moment, perspiration beading under her arms and on her palms. She had forgotten how hot even the mornings in August were. Spending most of her time in one of the few Tennessee prisons with air-conditioning, she had forgotten a lot about being outside. Like how the air smelled when it wasn't surrounded by a towering fence. How different the sky appeared when you viewed it from between trees instead of from behind the bars of a tiny window.

As she had known it would be, the double-doored entry to the church was unlocked. She opened one side and walked in. The air was cooler. Apparently air-conditioning had been added since her last visit.

But the smell had not changed.

Old, dank. Her father had bought the pews from a salvage place. The seller claimed they came from a two-hundred-year-old church in northern Tennessee.

Marcus was doing the same thing she had watched her father do a thousand times, ensuring the hymnals and Bibles were tucked into the racks on the backs of the pews. No one who needed one or both should be without. Not that her father had ever preached straight from the Bible. Instead, he had twisted the words to suit his own purposes. Funny how no one ever seemed to notice.

Or maybe they were simply afraid to mention it.

She had mentioned it plenty of times. Likely another of the reasons her father had hated her so.

The floor creaked with her first step inside as if the building itself was offended by her presence.

Marcus looked up. The pleasant expression he had been wearing vanished.

"Blasphemy," he bellowed.

She kept walking toward him. "Probably." She glanced up. "I expect the roof to fall in any second."

"Leave this church!" He pointed to the door. "I will not have the likes of you desecrating this house of God."

Cece laughed, could not help herself. "God has never been any part of this, Marcus."

He began to move toward her then. Cece stilled. Let him come. She refused to be afraid.

"You murdered our father." His tone simmered with hatred and disgust.

"You know I did not. You lied and so did Sierra. The only thing I want to know is why? Both of you hated him as much as I did. If you say you didn't, you're lying."

Fury twisted his lips. "You are the liar. Father knew what you were when he cast you out."

This man was her brother. How could he look at her with such sheer hatred and not the slightest flicker of basic human compassion?

"What've you done to Levi?"

"Levi has finally come to God." Marcus was close enough that he towered over her and had to glower down at her to look her in the eye. "I will not allow you to alter his course. Go back to the devil where you belong."

Cece peered up at him. "You know what I think? I think you killed our father. Look at all you had to gain. His church, his house. You came out with everything, Marcus. I wonder why the police didn't consider that."

"Foul bitch," he snarled. "You know Sierra and I had confirmed alibis."

"You two fooled everyone back then—except me. I'm going to set the record straight, Marcus. I will find the truth. This time you and Sierra won't be able to stop me."

"What is she doing here?"

Cece's gaze flew to the woman walking down that long center aisle. *Sierra.* Cece tried her best not to show how seeing her sister sucker-punched her, but she wasn't entirely successful. Some betrayals couldn't be so easily forgotten.

"Sierra." Cece drew in a big breath and steadied herself. "I was just telling Marcus how I'm looking for the truth. Why don't you help me find it?"

Sierra glared at their older brother. "What is she talking about, Marcus?"

Inside, where no one could see, Cece smiled.

"Get out," Marcus roared. "I won't have you here when the followers start to arrive."

"You shouldn't have come back, Cece," Sierra warned. "No one wants you here."

"When I find what I'm looking for," Cece said, "I'll be out of here so fast your head will spin. But I'm not going anywhere until then."

"Watch yourself, sister," Marcus mused with fire in his eyes. "There are many who wish you ill. I work diligently to keep my followers on the right track but I can't be expected to keep them all on the proper path."

"I'm aware," Cece assured him. "But your followers aren't going to stop me."

"God will take care of you, Cece," Sierra warned. "If I were you, I would be very afraid."

"Funny," Cece tossed back. "I'm not afraid at all."

She turned her back on the two and started toward the door.

Let them stew on that for a while.

Her brother started to pray. Sierra did the same.

Cece rolled her eyes.

DEACON PACED BACK AND FORTH, his gaze hardly leaving the entrance of the so-called church. He should never have allowed her to go in there alone. But she was right, her brother was far more likely to talk to her without an outsider around.

How had he stumbled so badly so far? He had been trained never to allow a civilian to walk into danger. Keeping her safe should have been a priority above all else—including solving the case. But it wasn't because he wanted the truth no matter the cost to her or anyone else.

She'd been found guilty of killing her own father. A woman like that wouldn't think twice about killing Deacon's partner.

Except now he wasn't so sure she had killed anyone.

He had waited a long time for this opportunity, had put his career and life on hold. Now he was riddled with second thoughts and uncertainty.

A car pulled into the lot, then another. He scanned the faces, shot another look at the door. What the hell was she doing in there? If the place filled with the older brother's followers anything could happen.

Before the thought fully formed in his brain Deacon had started for the entrance.

He was about to take the two steps up to the stoop when the door flew open and she stormed out.

"I'm done here," she said to him.

He nodded. "Okay."

They walked back to his truck amid curious stares from the ones who did not recognize Cece and hate-filled glares from those who did. He opened her door and waited for her to settle in the seat before he went around to the other side and climbed in behind the wheel.

"You recognize any of these people?"

"Some of them," she said as he backed away from the growing cluster of vehicles.

"Did you see Levi?"

"No. I think they've got him hidden away somewhere. Probably at the house."

"Do you mean against his will?"

She waited until he had pulled out onto the road and turned back to her before she nodded. "I believe so. I know Levi. He wouldn't become one of them. Not for any reason. He might pretend if he had to, but he would never do it for real."

"You think we should talk to Sheriff Tanner?" He asked this knowing full well she would say no. Like him, her plans didn't include playing by the rules. Involving the authorities required playing by the rules.

"Tanner can't help with Marcus." She stared out the window at the passing landscape. "Marcus and his followers consider themselves above the law. They answer only to God and to their interpretation of his word. Besides, they're too careful to make a mistake in front of anyone like the sheriff."

He braked for the stop sign at an intersection. "Like I told you before, I'm ready to help. What would you like to do next?"

She stared at him for a long moment. Guilt assaulted him again at the idea of how young she looked...how innocent. But she wasn't innocent. Was she? He had totally lost his perspective during the past forty or so hours. He wasn't sure how to get it back.

"I want to go to the house."

"Heading there now." He flipped on the left turn signal and checked for oncoming traffic.

"No. I mean the house where I grew up."

He pushed the turn signal back to the neutral position. "To go onto your brother's property would be trespassing."

She shook her head. "It'll be breaking and entering because I'm going inside the house."

Deacon opted not to try and talk her out of the decision.

But one thing was certain—if she was going in, so was he.

## Chapter Eight

The house where Cece grew up was a large two-story farm-style home set back in the woods on a forty-acre piece of property her father had inherited from his father. About five acres around the house were cleared for the yard and a massive garden. Their family had never raised their own livestock. Fresh milk, eggs and meat had been purchased from local farmers or provided by followers. Her father had lived by the philosophy that a man should focus on what he was good at and leave the rest to someone else.

Mason Winters had never been good at anything but conning people into believing the garbage he doled out as gospel. In Cece's opinion, it was a miracle no one had killed him long before she was supposed to have done the deed.

Right around this bend in the mile-long drive would be the house. If they drove any closer, anyone at the house would see them. To the right, just through those woods, was the church. It seemed farther when driving from the house to the church or vice versa, but through the woods it wasn't far at all.

She turned to the man behind the wheel, who so far had gone along with her scheme without balking. "You should probably stay in the truck. Me deciding to break the law is one thing, but I can't expect you to do the same."

Deacon stared at her as if she had lost her mind. Quite possibly she had. This was a risk. If Marcus caught her here, he would have her stoned or tortured in some other heinous manner rather than call the police. He would swear she had done something terrible and that he was only defending himself. She would either be dead or back in prison.

Which meant she could not get caught.

"Listen to me."

Deacon's words pulled her attention from those troubling thoughts to the man who'd spoken. This was the moment when he would tell her that if she went any further he was out. Completely understandable. He wasn't an outlaw or ex-con and she was. Her reputation was already a disaster. She had little to lose.

"The house," he went on, "belongs to Marcus now, right?"

She nodded. "He inherited it, yes. The house and the church. The one contingency is that he must always take care of his siblings—as long as they stay in the church. Levi and I were out of luck. Not that I wanted any of it. If I had inherited the place, I would have burned it down."

Before this was over, she might anyway.

"Did your father have guards when he was alive?

Anyone who watched after the house when he was away?"

"Not as far as I know."

"All right." He looked around. "I'm going to back into that narrow side road over there. I can park out of sight from the house or anyone who turns onto the driveway."

The side road he meant wasn't really a road. It was just a track that had formed over the years from the people who turned around in that spot when they realized they had taken the wrong road or changed their mind about visiting Reverend Winters. Cece had used that spot a few times herself. Usually when she needed to sneak back into the house for something she had left behind.

Once Deacon had backed into the clearing, he said, "I'll follow you as you approach the house, but I'll stay in the woods out of sight."

Considering all that Marcus had said to her in the church it was probably a good idea. He hated her. Sierra did, as well. It made Cece furious that she felt sad at the idea. She shouldn't care and somehow she still did. Wouldn't it be nice to cut them out of her heart entirely?

"Okay, if you think that's the best way."

"I do. What're you looking for, besides Levi?"

"I'm not sure. Maybe nothing beyond Levi. It's not like I think they'll have evidence of my innocence lying around. Or evidence of their own guilt, for that matter. I just need to look."

Her instincts wouldn't let go of the idea that there was something she needed to see.

She reached for the door handle.

"Remember, if you run into trouble—"

"I know," she said as she opened the door. "Scream."

"You got it."

Cece reached down deep for her courage, stepped out of the woods and started toward the house. As she rounded that curve and the house came into view, she immediately spotted two men. Both wore jeans and Salvation Survivalists tees. She didn't recognize either one. Well, well, her brother had decided guards were necessary.

The only reason to hire guards was if there was something worth guarding.

Had Marcus found out Levi visited her and decided to imprison him?

Deacon was trailing her. She felt confident he had spotted the guards, as well.

Standing on the porch, the two watched as she approached. They were armed. Rifles hung from straps draped over their shoulders. Thankfully, the rifles stayed on their shoulders as she approached. She had no desire to get herself shot.

When she was ten or so yards from the porch, she waved. "Hey. Is Levi home?"

The two men stared at her as if they weren't sure they should acknowledge her existence, much less speak to her.

"Marcus said he had stayed home sick today. I thought I'd check on him."

The taller of the two looked at his watch. His instinct, she suspected, was to call Marcus. But he couldn't. The church service was already underway.

"I'll ask him," the other guy said. "See if he's feeling up to company."

Anticipation seared through her veins. She was going in. At least, as long as Levi was there, and the man had basically said he was. "Thanks, I appreciate it."

The one who had checked his watch stayed on the porch and watched her while the other one went inside. She reminded herself to breathe but her lungs wouldn't cooperate. The service lasted a couple of hours, considering confessions and healings and all that other nonsense, so she had some time.

All she needed was inside.

Maybe she would have a chance to talk some sense into Levi.

As if the thought had summoned him, he appeared at the door, the guard behind him. He stared at her for a moment before he moved. Then he stormed across the porch and down the steps. He did not stop until he was standing toe to toe with her.

"What're you doing here?" he demanded.

She flinched. His voice was hard and unforgiving.

"I came to see you."

He stuck his face in hers and whispered fiercely. "Meet me at the shack in twenty minutes." Louder, he added, "You cannot be here! You are not one of us anymore." He backed up a step. "Leave and never come back."

Cece hesitated, her brain reluctant to absorb what was happening.

"I said get out of here!" he shouted.

She fell back a step.

Levi turned back to the house. To the guards he said, "If she ever tries to come back here again, escort her to the road."

Cece could not bring herself to turn around until Levi disappeared into the house once more. Then she turned and ran. No matter that he had told her to meet him at the shack, the rest of his words shook her to the core.

He was the one person in her family she had always been able to count on. Was it possible he really was one of them now?

She thought of the shack and how he had said to meet him there.

Maybe not. She could hang onto hope for a little while longer.

Deacon was already standing at the truck when she made it back there.

"Let's get out of here," he said, his face dark with fury.

If he had not heard Levi's message about meeting him at the shack, hopefully the others hadn't either.

"We have one more stop." She explained what Levi had whispered to her as they climbed into his truck.

"Where?" He didn't sound entirely convinced.

"It's an old tumbledown shack where we used to play as kids. I think it's actually on the neighboring property, but that never stopped us from using it."

After a couple of false starts she finally directed him down the right dirt road. Narrow, crowded on both sides by the forest, the road only led as far as the branch of the creek that crossed a portion of both properties. Fed by an underground stream, there was always water running in the creek—even during the hottest part of the year, like now.

The sound of the trickling water was soothing to her frazzled nerves. She had loved exploring these woods as a kid. They were the only pleasant memories she had after her mother's death. Deacon locked up his truck and moved along the side of the creek with her.

"There's a point where we have to cross to the other side." She hoped that fallen tree trunk was still sturdy enough to act as a bridge or they would be getting wet.

"You have any reason to doubt his motives for meeting you here?"

"No. If he had wanted to hurt me he would have had the guards take me in the house and keep me until Marcus came home."

"Valid point."

It was a good half mile before they reached the crossing point. Neither she nor Deacon had spoken after that initial burst of conversation. Sound carried in the woods. No one wanted to end up a target.

"I'll go first," Deacon suggested. "If it'll hold me, it'll hold you."

"If you're sure." She seriously appreciated his need to play the part of the gentleman. Part of her worried about him tiring of seeing after her. She was really starting to like his company for far more than his gallantry.

*So not smart, Cece.*

He adjusted his hat and stepped up onto the old log. About midway across it shifted and Cece's breath caught. Then he was on the other side.

"You think you can handle the pressure?" he asked.

"Get real. I did this a million times as a kid."

She took a breath and stepped up onto the log. Without hesitating, she moved across the length of it and hopped down on the other side.

"What did I tell you?"

He grinned. "Like riding a bike, huh?"

"Exactly." Speaking of that, she had to get her driver's license renewed. Tomorrow, she decided. No putting it off. Her job search had to start tomorrow, as well as reporting in with her probation officer.

The shack wasn't far once they were across the creek. It looked deserted and ready to fall in. Funny, when they were kids it had seemed so big and so cool. Like a pirate's stronghold or a gangster's hideout.

"Is that it?"

She nodded. "It's been a while since I was here."

Before she reached the shack, Levi stepped from behind it. He glared at Deacon and then at her. "What the hell are you doing, Cece?"

"I could ask you the same thing." All the anger she had been holding back since walking through those gates at the prison and finding no one waiting for her ignited inside her. "You were supposed to pick me up.

Do you have any idea how it felt to wait and wait and finally realize that no one was coming?"

"I'm sorry. Marcus wouldn't let me."

"Oh, so Marcus is your lord and master now?" She shook her head. "How did this happen, Levi?"

"First…" Her little brother glowered at her. "Who the hell is this?"

"A friend." She refused to tell him anything else. He had no right to demand anything from her.

"You think I'm going to talk in front of this *friend*?"

She was grateful Deacon kept quiet. "I trust him completely. You can trust him, too. He's helping me." When Levi would have argued, she added, "He kept Ricky and his friends from doing no-telling-what to me last night." She pointed to Deacon. "He stopped the two guys who planned to burn me out the night before. Oh, and did I mention that he kept a herd of Marcus's zombies from stoning me outside Ollie's?"

It wasn't until that moment, standing there staring at her little brother and recounting all that had happened in less than forty-eight hours, that the landslide of emotions hit her. She started to cry and she couldn't stop. No matter that she wanted to. No matter that she was embarrassing the hell out of herself. No matter that she hated the weakness. She. Could. Not. Stop.

"Cece, I'm sorry." Levi wrapped his arms around her. "I am so sorry. I messed up again."

She shuddered with the sobs rocking through her weary body. She was so tired of all of it. She should just leave and never look back.

But then she would never be free of this millstone. And all her grandmother had done would be for naught.

Levi drew back from her, held her by the shoulders. "After I came to see you the last time, I decided I was going to try and find the truth to save you the trouble. I know how much you want to prove your innocence." He exhaled a big breath. "It's just taken me longer than I expected."

Cece swiped at her eyes. "What're you talking about? This is too dangerous. You shouldn't be trying to fool Marcus. He's capable of anything, including killing you, you know that."

"I'm getting close, Cece. I heard him and Sierra talking the other night. She was telling him that he had to do something or you would figure it all out."

The words gave her pause. "Figure out what?"

"I don't know yet. For the first couple of weeks I was there they were real careful not to say anything around me or to leave me alone at the house. But they're loosening up now. Today was the first time I was ever able to stay at the house alone."

"What about the guards?"

He shook his head. "They don't come inside. I'm going through the house one room at a time looking for whatever I can find."

"It's too dangerous. Just forget it and come home with me." She did not want to lose her little brother. She had lost everyone else she cared about. She could not lose him, too. Nothing else was as important as his safety.

"Just let me do this. Let me keep listening and look-ing. When I have something, I'll come to you. Until then, you stay away from Marcus and Sierra. They're crazy, Cece." His eyes were wide with worry. "I mean, like, freaky crazy. I think Sierra might be on some sort of drugs. All she talks about is how she was daddy's princess and everybody better start treating her like one."

Obviously there was no talking him out of this. "Just Don't do anything too risky."

...ise."

Cece hugged him hard. "I can't lose you," she whis-pered against his ear.

"I better get back." He drew away and smiled at her. "You look good, Cece. A little pale, but good."

She slugged him on the shoulder. "You know how to sweet-talk a girl."

He glanced at Deacon. "I don't know about this guy, though."

"I do," Cece assured him.

They hugged some more and then went their sepa-rate ways.

Cece could not talk as she and Deacon walked back to his truck. Her emotions were too raw. Too full, press-ing against her breastbone.

When they were on the road headed toward home, she could not hold back anymore. She started to cry again. God, how she hated blubbering this way.

This time it was Deacon who held her. He pulled over to the side of the road and pulled her into his arms.

He held her until she had cried herself out. Until there were no more tears left.

And then he took her home.

"YOU REALLY DID not have to go to all this trouble."

Deacon grinned. "I'm not exactly a chef but I always prided myself in making a hell of a grilled cheese sandwich."

She nibbled another bite. "The extra cheese took a fect."

Deacon picked up his tea and took a swallow. "I'm glad you were able to see Levi today. I know you were worried about him."

He had considered several ways to bring up the subject again but he had put it off. She had been so torn up after the visit with her younger brother, he'd felt damned sorry for her.

He wasn't supposed to. Hated that he did, but he wasn't heartless.

Apparently, the girl he had thought was fully capable of killing another human wasn't entirely heartless, either. No one without a heart could cry like that.

"Me, too. But I'm worried about him. He wants to be my hero but I'm so worried he will get himself killed."

"You believe Marcus and his followers are capable of murder?"

She nodded and stared down at her sandwich.

"Cece? What's going on?" The lady had something on her mind. Something she was worried about telling him. Anticipation drummed in his chest. "You should know by now you can talk to me. I'm on your side in

# "FAST FIVE" READER SURVEY

Your participation entitles you to:
## ✳ 4 Thank-You Gifts Worth Over $20!

## *Complete the survey in minutes.*

## Get **2 FREE** Books

Your Thank-You Gifts include **2 FREE BOOKS** and **2 MYSTERY GIFTS**. There's no obligation to purchase anything!

*See inside for details.*

Dear Reader,

Since you are a lover of our books, your opinions are important to us... and so is your time.

That's why we made sure your **"FAST FIVE" READER SURVEY** can be completed in just a few minutes. Your answers to the five questions will help us remain at the forefront of women's fiction.

And, as a thank-you for participating, we'd like to send you **4 FREE THANK-YOU GIFTS!**

Enjoy your gifts with our appreciation,

*Pam Powers*

## To get your
## 4 FREE THANK-YOU GIFTS:

✳ Quickly complete the "Fast Five" Reader Survey
and return the insert.

## "FAST FIVE" READER SURVEY

**1** Do you sometimes read a book a second or third time? ○ Yes ○ No

**2** Do you often choose reading over other forms of entertainment such as television? ○ Yes ○ No

**3** When you were a child, did someone regularly read aloud to you? ○ Yes ○ No

**4** Do you sometimes take a book with you when you travel outside the home? ○ Yes ○ No

**5** In addition to books, do you regularly read newspapers and magazines? ○ Yes ○ No

**YES!** I have completed the above Reader Survey. Please send me my 4 FREE GIFTS (gifts worth over $20 retail). I understand that I am under no obligation to buy anything, as explained on the back of this card.

❑ I prefer the regular-print edition
182/382 HDL GNSC

❑ I prefer the larger-print edition
199/399 HDL GNSC

| | |
|---|---|
| FIRST NAME | LAST NAME |

ADDRESS

| | |
|---|---|
| APT.# | CITY |

| | |
|---|---|
| STATE/PROV. | ZIP/POSTAL CODE |

all this. You can trust me on that one. I won't let you down."

Three lies in a row. He was on a roll.

Funny thing was, they didn't *feel* like lies.

"There was a man." She clasped her hands together, her forearms braced on her knees. "Back when everything went to hell. His name was K.C., you know, like the initials."

Shock radiated through Deacon. K.C. was the cover name Jack had been using. K for Kelley and C for Charlie, his kids.

"He came around my grandmother's house a few times asking questions. I think he was some kind of undercover agent or..." She shrugged. "I don't know. Anyway, my grandmother wouldn't talk to him. She warned me not to, either. She said he was trouble and that we did not need any trouble. She was trying to keep a low profile because my father was on one of his rampages."

"Rampages?" It was all Deacon could do not to grab her and shake her. He needed answers and it felt as if he was so damned close.

"Every so often he would decide I was his daughter and he wanted me back. He would give my grandmother hell. I suspected she was giving him money to get him to stay away from me, but she would never admit as much."

"So you never spoke to this K.C.?" He reminded himself to breathe. To keep the tension inside where she couldn't see.

"He caught up with me once at the diner where I worked as a waitress. It was the only time he tried to talk to me. I guess my grandmother put the fear of God in him because he never approached me before or after that day."

"What happened?"

"He asked me if I was ever aware of my father being involved with a group known as Resurrection. I had heard of them. A secret society of preppers— you know, the doomsday people. I told him the truth, that if my father had anything to do with them, I knew nothing about it. The members don't want anyone to know who they are, you know? I heard my father say once that it was because when Armageddon comes they don't want the fools who aren't prepared to come to them for help."

"Did this K.C. seem okay? Upset or angry by your answer?"

"He was nice. Kind, you know, in a fatherly sort of way. Not that I had ever had a role model to go by, but he was very nice. I didn't understand why my grandmother was so afraid of him. Anyway, I never saw him again after that. I guess I couldn't give him what he needed so he moved on. He seemed really intent on learning about my father's connection to that group."

"You're certain your father wasn't part of them?"

"I don't think so, but I really tried to stay clear of him. Even before I left home, I avoided him like the plague. We hated each other."

"Would Levi know? He stayed home after you left, right? You think he was approached by this K.C. guy?"

She searched his face, his eyes. "I don't know. He

never mentioned the prepper stuff or the man. Do you know him?"

This was the moment. If he lied and later she found out—and she would—she wouldn't forgive him. If he told the truth, she could balk here and now.

He was too close to take the risk.

"I'm just looking at all the possibilities." When she still looked suspicious, he posed a question that he thought would erase that look from her eyes. "You think this K.C. could have had something to do with your father's murder?"

She frowned. "I don't know. I never considered the possibility. I guess it's possible." She turned back to Deacon. "But he was really nice, so I don't know."

Nice.

Really nice.

The realization that this woman—the woman he had studied and obsessed over for months—knew nothing about Jack or his disappearance hit him square between the eyes.

She wasn't the one.

He had despised her for so long. Hated her, actually. Dreamed of taking her down. Those people who had thrown stones at her that first day were likely there because he had leaked the date and time of her exit from prison. He had wanted her to be humiliated, shamed.

And he had been wrong.

"I'm sorry." The words choked out of him before he could stop them.

She blinked. "Why are you sorry?"

Before he could answer, she reached for his hand and took it in her own. "You've been so nice to me, Deacon. I'm not sure how I could have gotten through all this without your help. Thank you."

He managed a smile though he felt sick—sick at what he had done. "You don't need to thank me."

"I know you didn't want to kiss me when I asked. But is it okay if I kiss you? On the cheek, I mean? To show my appreciation."

"Sure."

She stretched toward him and kissed him on the jaw. Her lips were soft, like a butterfly's wings against his skin.

She drew away quickly, shot to her feet as if she intended to run. "I should clean up the mess in the kitchen."

"I'll help." He stood, reached for his plate.

"You did the cooking," she argued.

"At least let me watch."

"Fine." She picked up her plate and glass and led the way over to the sink.

He watched as she filled it with hot water. There was no dishwasher. When she'd wiped down the counter and the stovetop, he decided to dig a little deeper into the older brother.

"Based on what I know about Marcus, he never married. No kids."

She paused, her hands deep in the sudsy water. "There was a girl back when he was in high school, but they broke up and as far as I know there wasn't another serious relationship."

"You think he has been too focused on building his followers? Or maybe what he really wants, he can't have because of his beliefs. Maybe he fell for someone who isn't a follower?"

"It's possible, I guess, but Marcus is so uptight. I can't see him doing anything like that. He would die first. He's just a loner, I think. He stopped having friends and participating in extracurricular activities at school when he was really young, like twelve or thirteen. He was that devoted to following in our father's footsteps.

"He was the only teenage boy I knew who spent all his free time with the elderly of the congregation. Every time one of them would pass away he would lock himself in his room for days. Maybe he used up all his compassion when he was young and had none left by the time he was an adult. He certainly never had any for me."

Deacon picked up a tea towel and reached for the plate she had rinsed. "What about Sierra? Was she similarly devoted?"

Cece shook her head. "When we were little kids, she adored me. The three of us, including Levi, played all the time and we were happy. As happy as kids in our situation could be. But then about the time our father kicked me out, she changed. It was like she suddenly hated me. She hardly left the house. It wasn't until she finally had a boyfriend that I started to see her around town again. She still had nothing to say to me, but at least she acted somewhat normal. Whenever I'd ask Levi he would only say that she was nuts. He thinks she was taking drugs even back then."

Her family had been devastated after their mother's death. Deacon was beginning to think it had more to do with Marcus and Sierra than it did with the father.

He watched her rinse the sink and dry her hands.

When had this investigation become about her and her family instead of his partner?

# Chapter Nine

Cece watched as the number on the digital readout changed from 21 to 22, then she stared at the blue tag with the number 25 in her hand.

Apparently the first week of the month was the busy time at the driver's license renewal office. She sighed. She still didn't feel comfortable driving, but she supposed that would come with time. Living in the small-town South, it was necessary. There were no handy buses or trains to take you around town.

Deacon had offered to bring her but she had decided she needed some time alone. She glanced around the crowded lobby. Not that she was alone, by any means, but so far no one had recognized her. Basically she was alone. Everyone in the lobby was either scrolling on their cell phones or chatting with their neighbor in the next chair.

Since Cece had no cell phone and didn't know either of the older men seated next to her, she just sat there. If she was very still maybe they wouldn't notice her and strike up a conversation. It was human nature to ask about school, jobs, kids, the everyday sorts of things. Telling anyone she had spent her college years in prison and had no boyfriend, much less a husband and kids, was not exactly an acceptable icebreaker. The person asking would no doubt regret having done so.

Her mind drifted to the new images imprinted in her memory of her neighbor lingering in her kitchen, staring out the window over the sink, a steaming cup of coffee in his hand. She had stared at him a good long while before making her presence known this morning. The way the jeans he wore molded to his body. The way his shirt stretched over his shoulders. His shaggy brown hair curled around his collar.

Some part of her wondered why this stranger would go so far out of his way to help her. Did he have nothing better to do? Was he simply bored? She wanted him to be exactly what he appeared to be—the stranger next door who liked playing the role of Good Samaritan.

But another part of her worried that she was making a mistake. She didn't really know him. Did not know his true motive.

Yet she wanted to know him…wanted to do things with him. She felt heat rush up her cheeks. She covertly glanced at the people around her as if she had said the words out loud rather than thought them.

It was true, though. She wanted to kiss him, to be kissed by him. She wanted him to touch her, to show her all the ways a man could pleasure a woman. Her one and only sexual experience had been awkward and bumbling with that jerk Ricky Olson. Just kissing Deacon on the cheek had made her pulse race.

That he genuinely seemed interested in helping her with her search for the truth just made the idea of—

"That's you."

Cece jumped. The man to her right gestured to the number she held and then to the display. She forced her lips into a polite smile. "Oh, thank you."

She hurried to the counter and presented the required documentation. The clerk informed her that since her license had been expired for so long she would need to retake the driver's test. This was not something she had come prepared to do, but there it was. She could either do it now or come back.

Now was as good a time as any.

Once the written part was over, the administering officer climbed into her truck and advised her of the route for the road test. Cece drove. She made the turns he requested and parallel parked as best she could in front of the federal courthouse. The officer said little else to her, only giving her the directions. By the time they returned to the office, her nerves were shot and she had no idea if she had passed his test.

He led the way back to the counter and gave a paper to the clerk who had waited on her when she first arrived. The woman smiled. "Congratulations, Miss Winters. You passed. Stand right over there on that red X and I'll take your picture for the license."

The photo and remaining paperwork took only a couple of minutes. Cece left with a paper version of her new license. The final version would arrive in the mail in ten to fourteen days.

Cece stopped by the insurance office and updated the information in her file with her new driver's license number. Next was the visit to her parole officer. That part was surprisingly easy. The man, Mr. Berringer, was nice. He was older, sixtyish, and very kind. He made Cece feel as if she was a real person who mattered, not a recently released murderer. She was grateful. Funny how she found that sort of kindness in the least-expected places. The sheriff, the chief of police, they had all been exceedingly nice to her. Like the man next door.

Afterward, rather than going straight home, she decided to stop by the cemetery to visit her grandmother's grave. She made a quick stop at the florist and bought her grandmother's favorite roses.

At the cemetery she walked through the aisles of headstones until she found the right one. Though she had not been here for her grandmother's funeral, she had been present for her grandfather's. Emily Broward was interred next to the man she had loved her whole life.

Cece knelt down and placed the flowers against the headstone. "Hey, Gran."

Emily Broward had preferred Gran to Grandmother. Cece smiled as she thought of how her grandmother had never failed to look less than perfectly put together. Her hair was always just so, the makeup, the outfit. Even when she was gardening she looked ready to drop everything and run to the country club. The one person in the world she had loved as much as her husband was her only child, Cece's mother. She had always said her grandkids came in a close second, especially after Cece's mother died.

For as long as Cece could remember, everyone believed that Emily Broward was partial to Cece because she looked so much like her mother, but that wasn't the real reason. Cece was the one who spent the most time with her. She took every possible opportunity to be with her grandmother. Helped her in any way she needed. Then Cece had moved in after her father kicked her out. Of course they were close. Her grandmother had not chosen Cece over anyone else; Cece had chosen her.

Movement a few yards away drew her attention. The blonde woman walking the cemetery with her German shepherd looked vaguely familiar. Cece watched her until she was close enough to get a good look at her face.

Rowan DuPont. The undertaker's daughter.

Cece didn't really know her—not personally. But she had seen her on the news. First because she'd published a book that gained her national attention. Seemed funny to know someone from her small hometown who was so famous. Then she had seen the news about Rowan's father being murdered by a serial killer who was a close friend. Cece vividly remembered Mr. DuPont. He had taken care of her grandfather. He'd also taken care of her mother, but she didn't remember as much about that funeral. She'd only been six at the time.

Rowan's mother had died when she was young, too. She had hung herself right there in the funeral home only a few months after Rowan's twin sister drowned.

Their gazes collided and the other woman smiled. Cece smiled back. They both had plenty of tragedy in their histories. If Rowan DuPont could pick up the pieces and move on, maybe there was hope for Cece.

Rowan and her dog walked out of the cemetery and disappeared down the block. She, too, had come back to Winchester after a great tragedy. Somehow she had found a way to survive the rumors and the gossip.

Cece wasn't sure she wanted to try. She just wanted the truth. Then she wanted to be anywhere but here.

"You always could fool her."

Cece's gaze shot up to meet her sister's. Sierra stood six or seven feet away, her face full of accusation.

Pushing to her feet, Cece held her contemptuous glare. "Fooling people is your specialty, Sierra, not mine. I guess you never outgrew that childish habit."

Sierra glared at her, her raven-black hair and equally black eyes so unlike Cece's own pale coloring. "You should move on, Cece. You can't change the past. You did what you did and no one is ever going to believe your lies claiming otherwise. You took him away from all of us."

Cece took a step toward Sierra. She refused to allow her little sister to use her intimidation tactics anymore. "I did not kill him, Sierra. Maybe it was you. You were the one still stuck under his thumb. The princess he doted on all the time. The one who did everything he said. Maybe you got tired of his rules."

Hatred filled Sierra's black eyes. "You couldn't possibly understand how much I loved him. He was everything to me."

Now that was about as far from the truth as could be gotten. "Liar. You hated him as much as I did."

Sierra laughed. "Whatever my true feelings, I was so much smarter than you, sister. I did not go around telling people how much I hated him the way you did. Even if you hadn't been found with blood all over you, everyone would still have believed you killed him."

"Maybe it was Marcus. He was the one who had the most to gain. He took over the house, the church. It's all about him now."

"I'll be sure to tell him you said so." Sierra stepped toward her now. "You know he hates you for killing our father. He loved him so. Worshipped him, really. He never wanted you to get out of jail. He still hasn't forgiven you. We both know how Marcus always took care of the sick and dying of Father's flock. Maybe he'll take care of you when your time comes, Cece. I would watch my back if I were you."

"Well…" Cece wasn't surprised in the least about her brother's feelings. Marcus had always been obsessed with their father. "You give him my best. And don't worry. I will be watching. I'm watching you both."

"Maybe it's Levi you should be worried about. He would have done anything for you. Maybe he killed Daddy and you took the fall for him." Sierra smiled. "I wonder if Marcus has ever considered that possibility. It is rather strange that Levi finally wanted back in the fold when it came time for you to be released. Maybe he's afraid the truth will finally come out."

Cece moved in toe to toe with her. "You leave Levi out of this. He had nothing to do with what happened to that old bastard. I'm just glad he's dead. I wish it *had* been me who shoved that knife into his loathsome chest over and over."

Fury whipped across Sierra's face. "I guess prison didn't rehabilitate you at all. You're still the same heartless bitch you were when we were kids."

"I'm not heartless, Sierra, I'm just not a fool. Mason Winters was a con artist and a pathetic excuse for a father. I'm glad he's dead."

"Maybe you'll join him soon, sister. I know a lot of people want to see the end of you."

"Maybe," Cece allowed. "But I will know the truth first. You can't stop me from finding it." She held her thumb and forefinger an inch apart. "I'm this close."

Sierra turned to go but then hesitated. "Just so you know, no one is going to bring you flowers when you're in the ground next to her." She glanced at their grandmother's headstone and then walked away.

Cece hugged her arms around herself and pressed her lips together. Nothing she could say or do would change how her sister felt. Didn't matter. All those years ago Cece had been so worried about her sister and her brothers and what was going to become of them.

She wasn't worried anymore. They could go to hell. Every damned one of them. All she wanted was the truth.

She said her goodbyes to her grandmother and headed back to the truck. When she rounded the cemetery gate and started up the sidewalk, she stalled. Her truck sat right where she had left it, at the curb next to the sidewalk. But the tires were flat. She hurried the last few yards and walked all the way around the vehicle. All four tires had been slashed. If she had not been so damned mad she might have cried.

Fortunately, the local co-op was able to take care of her tires. They were slashed—probably with a knife—in such a way that they couldn't be repaired. Cece used a portion of the money she had found in the books to have a new set installed and aligned. She had the oil changed while she was at it.

After she left the co-op, she stopped by a local staffing firm and filled out an application. Mr. Berringer had warned that having and keeping a job was not optional. It was required. However long she would be here, she had to try and proceed with a normal life.

She laughed as she drove home, the sound flowing out the open window as she drove. There was nothing normal about her life. Never had been, probably never would be.

By the time she arrived it was well past lunch, and she was hungry and emotionally drained. She grabbed the mail from the box and rolled the rest of the way down the drive. When she had parked she sifted through the mail. An envelope from the tax assessor's office snagged her attention. She opened it first.

Delinquent taxes. Lien.

A lien had been taken out against the house because of overdue taxes. This was the third notice.

She wanted to lay her head against the steering wheel and sob. She really did. This had been a really horrendous day. Instead, she twisted the key in the ignition to start the engine. She might as well go back to town and take care of this now.

The engine failed to turn over. A frown furrowed her brow. She tried again. Nothing but a *click, click, click*.

She dropped her head back against the seat. What now?

The only choice she had was to call Deacon and see if he was interested in coming to her rescue yet again.

Funny how the stranger next door had turned out to be the best neighbor she could possibly hope for.

A real hero.

CECE WAS SITTING on the top porch step when Deacon pulled into her driveway. She looked as if she had lost her best friend, except he knew she didn't have any friends. For all intents and purposes, she was completely alone in the world. An outcast.

One he had been certain was guilty of far more than she had gone to prison for. He worried now that he had made a mistake, but he wasn't ready to give her quite that much grace just yet. There were still questions. Questions for which he intended to have answers. At this point he was relatively certain she wasn't guilty of murdering her father or having anything to do with his partner's disappearance. But she had information.

Information he needed to solve that mystery once and for all.

"Nice tires," he said as he walked around her truck.

She pushed to her feet and descended the steps as if she were walking to the gallows. "Now if only the engine would work to roll those nice tires down the road."

"Sounds like the battery. Let's have a look." He raised the hood; she joined him as he surveyed the engine compartment.

"Let's clean these connections up a little and see if that helps." He went back to his truck and grabbed his toolbox.

"You think that might do it?"

"It can't hurt." He scraped the buildup from the connectors, one by one, and tapped them back into place. "Try starting it now."

She climbed in and did as he asked. The engine turned over but too slowly to start. She made a face and groaned.

"Let's go get a new battery. That'll most likely take care of the problem."

"What if it's not just the battery?"

He removed the connectors again, removed the battery. "Could be the alternator, but judging by the looks of this battery, this is likely the source of the trouble. They can test it to be certain."

After putting the battery in the back of his truck, he opened the passenger-side door and waited for her to get in.

"Can we stop at the tax assessor's office first?" She

held up a letter. "I guess no one remembered to pay the taxes."

"Should be an easy fix, as well."

"That might just salvage this really crappy day. Stopping by the cemetery turned out to be an unpleasant decision."

She looked so hopeful, he couldn't help the smile. "Hop in."

They were a mile or so down the road when she asked, "How has your day been?"

"A lot more boring than yours, apparently." He shot her a grin. "So tell me what happened at the cemetery."

She told him about her sister's visit. "You think she slashed your tires?"

"It was either her or a friend of hers."

"Do you really believe she or Marcus killed your father?"

"It wasn't Levi," she answered without answering his question. "He couldn't have done it. Based on what Sierra and Marcus said about me at trial and what I've seen since I got back, I wouldn't put anything past either of them."

"But it could have been another member of his following," Deacon countered. He had been thinking about that today. More than a few of his followers had fallen out with Mason Winters around the time of his murder. The man's popularity had been on the decline. The trouble was that many of his followers wanted to cling to him because he had started the church.

Those were the ones who would have gravitated to his son over anyone else. The son had, from all accounts, turned things around. Membership was on the rise and his congregation appeared to be loyal to a fault.

"Probably. I had been out of the church for a while at that point so I wasn't privy to the ongoing politics. The police investigated the possibility but not really well. I think they were satisfied that I killed him and didn't want to waste time."

She was likely right. "I was thinking about the man, the K.C. that you mentioned. I think you should talk to Levi about him. There may be a connection to who killed your father. Maybe his murder had something to do with that Resurrection group you were telling me about."

"It's worth a shot. Some of those extreme preppers are very territorial."

The quiet that followed warned him that she had something else on her mind.

"Have you ever been married, Deacon?" She made a face. "If you don't mind me asking."

"Never been married."

She looked surprised.

Before she could ask, he went on, "I guess I'm like your older brother. I never took the time to nurture a relationship."

"No kids?"

He shook his head. "My parents live in Nashville. I have a sister. No brothers. Several cousins and a half dozen or so aunts and uncles."

She smiled and he liked the way it made her green eyes sparkle. "Do you have big family get-togethers for the holidays?"

He slowed for a turn. "Sometimes."

"We never had those. My mother was an only child and my father had no association with any member of his family. One of his brothers came to his funeral. I think they're all in Memphis."

"Your father didn't approve of the holiday dinners and celebrations?"

"Not the way the average person does. His idea of a family get-together was him preaching some hellfire and brimstone sermon while we sat and listened avidly. If we blinked or looked away we were punished."

"Sounds like a great guy." Some people shouldn't have children.

More of that quiet.

"You can ask me whatever you like." Might as well let her off the hook.

"Have you decided what you're doing next? Is there a chance you'll be going back to Nashville or someplace like that?"

He pulled into a parking slot at the courthouse. "I'm not sure yet. Just taking my time and considering my options."

"Hopefully this won't take long." She reached for the door.

"Why don't I go with you?"

She searched his face for a moment. "Okay."

He got out and met her at the hood. There was a distinct possibility he was taking the protective thing too far. He opened the entrance door and followed her inside. A chance he was willing to take. In light of the trouble that kept showing up, he wasn't ready to let her out of his sight. He knew who had slashed her tires because he had been watching. The question was, why would her brother do that?

Levi was supposed to be the only one who cared about her.

Deacon watched as Cece showed the letter to the lady behind the counter. He noted the way the other woman looked at her, as if she were nothing—not worthy of standing in their midst. If Cece noticed she pretended not to. The clerk seemed reluctant to accept the cash Cece placed on the counter. Maybe she feared she had just printed it or earned it on the street corner selling drugs or herself.

By the time Cece finished her business and they walked out, he was fire-breathing angry on her behalf.

"Anything else you need to do while we're here?" He had to work at keeping his tone even.

"I think that's it other than the battery."

"There's a new diner in town. I've heard good things about it. After we pick up the battery, why don't we go for a late lunch and celebrate?"

"What're we celebrating?"

She looked so uncertain and yet so hopeful. He wanted to pull her into his arms and promise her it would all work out just fine.

What the hell was wrong with him? He had lost all perspective. But the real problem was that he no longer cared.

"Surprises," he offered. "Life is full of them."

## Chapter Ten

The diner wasn't really new. It was the same one that had been in Winchester as long as Cece could remember. She had worked here when she was a teenager…before she ended up in prison. Of course Deacon had no way of knowing that. The place had shut down ages ago and only recently reopened under new management.

When they had placed their orders, Cece said as much. "Working here was my first job."

He surveyed the place. "Well I'll be damned. Here I thought I was bringing you to someplace new."

The shiplap walls were white now instead of the stained wood color they had been when she was a kid. The red booths with the gold-speckled white tables were the same. The black-and-white tile floors were a little shinier. The long counter that served as a bar was still fronted by red leather-topped stools.

"It's the thought that counts, right?" She lifted her soda and took a sip. Tried to relax but that wasn't happening. Part of her worried that someone who remembered her would walk up to their table and make a scene. If it hadn't meant having to face the public every hour of every work day, she would have asked if waitresses were needed. Picking up where she'd left off would have been easy enough and maybe even allowed her to work her hours around a class schedule at nearby Motlow College.

"You started working here when you were in high school?"

He had the brownest eyes. Kind eyes. Not dark and cruel like her father's had been. She blinked away the thought. "Yes. My dad kicked me out and I didn't want to take advantage of my grandmother's kindness so I got a job here after school and on weekends. Bought my own clothes. Paid for my lunch at school. She said it wasn't necessary but that it was a good idea since staying busy would keep me out of trouble."

Too bad that part hadn't worked.

"Sounds like your grandmother was a really cool lady."

"She was. A fiery redhead like me and my mother. Green eyes, too." Cece smiled, remembering. "Smaller than me. She swore she was five feet tall but she wasn't. Maybe four-eleven. But she wasn't afraid of anything or anyone."

Except her father. Cece knew her grandmother had worried about the bastard trying to drag Cece back home before she turned eighteen. Two tough years. Cece hated that she had been the cause of those worrisome weeks and months for her grandmother. But Emily Broward had sworn she wouldn't have it any other way. She wanted Cece with her. To hell with the rest if they didn't recognize what an evil snake their father was. Her grandmother had truly been one of a kind.

As much as it pained her, she had thought Marcus was just as evil as his father. Sierra was too young and too much of a follower to understand, her grandmother had insisted. Levi waffled between sleeping over at their grandmother's and crawling back home. Cece had understood. He'd wanted the approval of his father and his older brother. Most young boys did. He hadn't recognized what they were. She hoped he did now.

She didn't want to lose Levi, too.

"I have a feeling you're a lot like your grandmother," Deacon said.

Cece smiled. "Maybe. Either way, I consider that a compliment."

"You said this man, K.C., came to your grandmother's house. Do you think she knew him? Maybe he talked to her when you were at school or at work."

She hadn't considered the idea. "It's possible, I guess."

"It seems too much of a coincidence that he was coming around about the same time your father was murdered. He may be related somehow to what happened."

She had wondered about that since she'd suddenly remembered him showing up those times. "I should start going through more of the files my attorney sent."

"I can help with that, if you'd like."

He had made the offer to help before. He certainly gave the impression of being sincere about it. But he still hadn't told her what he did for the federal government. Was it possible he did the same thing that man—the one who went by the name K.C.—did?

"Do you know that man? K.C.? Is that why you're asking about him?"

He held her gaze for a long while before answering. Cece felt her world shifting. She needed this man—this stranger—to be the real deal. A nice guy who lived next door. She absolutely did not want to learn he was some kind of creep or just some investigator using her for his own purposes. He'd admitted to having done some private investigations. Uneasiness started a slow crawl through her.

"Maybe. We have reason to believe he was someone else. A man we've been trying to find for a very long time."

There it was. The cold, hard truth.

"Is that why you've been so nice to me? So helpful?" Her heart pounded twice for every second that elapsed before he smiled and shook his head.

"Cece, I had no idea you'd ever met the man until you brought him up."

She closed her eyes and shook her head. "Sorry. I'm just so used to being let down."

He reached across the table and covered her hand with his own, sending warmth firing through her. "I'm sorry I didn't tell you I was looking for him when you first mentioned his alias."

"Alias?" She felt suddenly cold despite the warmth he had elicited.

"K.C. is an alias he used for going undercover."

"What's his real name?"

"I'm afraid I can't tell you that."

"But you think he was working on something related to the Resurrection doomsday preppers or whatever they are?"

He nodded. "We think so. Whatever he was doing, he's been missing since around the same time your father was murdered."

"Wow." She tried to remember the man's face, the words he'd said. "Do you think he's dead, too?"

"That's what we need to find out."

The waitress arrived with their burgers and fries. Deacon drew his hand away and Cece wished he was still holding onto her. The idea that she was in way over her head had her digging into the food in hopes of ignoring the new tension flooding her. Honestly, she hadn't realized how hungry she was until she smelled the food. She poured on the ketchup and devoured the fries first.

She caught Deacon watching her and felt embarrassed. "Sorry. I was starving and maybe trying to comfort myself."

He grinned. "Nothing wrong with that." He popped a fry into his mouth and chewed. "We all need a little comfort now and then."

She was suddenly afraid. Three days. She had known this man for three days and already she felt close to him, dependent on having him back her up. On him being here…with her.

She was a complete idiot.

She stared at her burger and suddenly felt sick. What if he wasn't who she believed he was? What if he was lying to her? Everyone except her grandmother had lied to her. She knew better than to trust.

And yet, somehow she trusted this man.

*Not smart, Cece.*

Apparently she had never been as smart as she should have been, otherwise she wouldn't have ended up spending most of her adult life so far in prison.

She watched Deacon as he bit off a chunk of his burger. He had great lips for a man. Classic square jaw. Perfect nose, not too big, not crooked. He was handsome and sexy and so nice.

Really nice.

Her grandmother had always said when something seemed too good to be true, it usually was.

Was this man another mistake? He surely seemed too good to be true.

DEACON SHUT OFF the engine and climbed out of Cece's old blue truck. "You are good to go." The new battery had taken care of the problem. According to the gauge on the truck, the alternator was charging. "You shouldn't have any more trouble."

"The guy at the tire shop said the brakes were still good." She stood watching him, her arms crossed over her chest.

He closed the driver's-side door and moved toward where she stood just outside the entrance to the makeshift garage that was actually a part of the barn. "You got something on your mind?"

"I was thinking we should go through those files. If your offer to help is still on the table."

He moved beyond the doors, pushed them shut. "Sure." He dropped the crosspiece into place that held the doors closed. "If you're certain you want me to help. I feel like you might have some doubts or misgivings about me."

No point allowing her uncertainty to build. He had made a couple of missteps and he needed to rectify the situation while it was still salvageable. Whatever else he thought about this woman, she was still his only connection to Jack. She could very well be one of the last people to see him before he disappeared. If she or anyone she knew had information that would help find him, Deacon had to pursue that route. No matter the cost.

That last part didn't sit right in his gut. He didn't want to be another of the people who'd hurt this woman.

"I trust you, Deacon." She smiled and he hated himself a little more. "I'm grateful for any and all help."

"Okay. Let's get to it."

She led the way inside the house. That he watched her hips sway with far too much interest was another reason to hate himself. But he was human. She was a gorgeous woman. Petite with soft curves. All that red hair that made him long to tangle his fingers in those silky curls. He wasn't alone in his fascination. She looked at him with a similar yearning. He had thought as much, but the way she'd stared at him in the diner had confirmed his instincts. She was attracted to him.

But then she was lonely. To let this mutual attraction go any farther would be taking advantage of her vulnerability and he did not want to go there. In his ten-year career he had never used sex as leverage or influence.

This was the first time he'd ever longed to do exactly that, whether it proved beneficial to his investigation or not.

In the living room, she settled on her knees next to the coffee table. "He had a copy of everything as far as I can tell. Arrest record. Witness interviews. Not that there were any actual witnesses to the murder, but people who knew him and who knew me."

"Character references and situational witnesses. That's the usual procedure when no one saw what really happened. The police build a scenario based on what they can find out about the people closest to the victim. In your case, you were at the scene—covered in his blood—so they started with you."

"Since they found what they wanted, they didn't look any further," she suggested.

He nodded. "From what you've told me and what Frasier showed me, it certainly seems that way."

She stared at the pages and pages lying on the table. "How can any of this tell us anything if it only shows what we already know?"

"There's always the chance that something someone said in an interview will mean something different to you than it did to the investigating officers or to Frasier or me." That was his only thought when he'd first reviewed the file with Frasier. The notes and statements provided little else in the way of support for her version of events.

"Oh." The frown that had creased her forehead relaxed. "I see. I think."

He wasn't so sure she did. "Let's make a list of people you would consider suspects in the murder of Mason Winters."

Cece shuffled the pages around and found the notepad she had been using. A pen and a pencil lay amid the pages. She grabbed the pencil and wrote *Suspects* across the top of the page. Her strokes were neat and fine with a dash of unique flair, the way a teenage girl would write. The reality that she'd never had the opportunity to move beyond the writing style she'd developed in high school was another reminder of what she'd lost. Eight years of learning, of becoming who she would be.

He forced away the thoughts and focused on the task at hand. "Who would you put at the top of the list? The person you believe had the most to gain by his death."

She hesitated only a moment before she wrote *Marcus Winters*. "He gained the church and most of our father's followers. He got the house. He has the power now. The admiration and respect."

"Okay, that's a start. Who's next?" He had his own ideas about that one but he wanted to hear her conclusions before he gave his own.

Another of those worrisome frowns lined her brow as she considered the question for a bit. "Sierra. She was a little wilder than me. She didn't like all his rules, but they had this bizarre daddy–daughter relationship. She was his princess and it was like sometimes she adored him and wanted his attention and sometimes she didn't. You never knew which Sierra you were going to get." She wrote her sister's name next.

Sierra would have been his second choice, as well.

"Was there anyone else among his followers who might have hoped to gain control of the church?"

"I don't think so." She tilted her head as if reconsidering. "There was this one man who came every Sunday and sat in the back. He never spoke to anyone. My father made it a point to know all of his followers. He was like a politician, he pretended to be friends with everyone. The fact that he never exchanged so much as a hello with the man was unusual. I told the police about him, but Marcus claimed I made him up."

"Do you remember his name?"

"I never knew his name, but he came into the diner once. It was the only time I ever saw him in town. He sat at one of my tables."

She fell silent, remembering.

"He ordered hot tea," she finally said. "No food, just the drink. He sat there for half an hour or so and watched me."

"Did you tell the police about this incident?"

She nodded. "I did but they blew it off." She shrugged. "I suppose it did sound as if I had made him up. I didn't know his name, and Marcus and anyone else they asked—assuming they asked anyone else— had no idea who or what I was talking about. It was an easy jump to conclude I was trying to shift focus from me."

"What did he look like?"

"Old. Maybe sixty-something. Heavy gray beard. Gray hair. Medium height, thin."

"How did he dress?"

"Overalls and plain plaid shirts, the button-up style. Boots. The hiking kind, not cowboy boots like you wear. That was another thing that made him stand out at the meetings. The followers wear very plain clothes, solid colors. The plaid shirt said all that needed to be said. He was not a follower."

"No hat?"

Her gaze narrowed. "There was a hat. Not a cowboy hat or straw hat. One of the felt kind, like a fedora. A really old one, like you see in those black-and-white movies."

"Eye color?"

She shook her head. "I don't know. I never looked that close. He made me nervous, sort of."

"He didn't say anything to you that time in the diner?"

"Just gave me his order."

"Was that close to the time your father was murdered?"

"Maybe a week before. I can't be sure. It didn't seem significant at the time and by the time it did, it was too late."

A thought occurred to Deacon. "Are there photographs from the trial in these files?" The files Frasier had showed to him hadn't contained any pictures. Deacon couldn't be sure, but by the time he'd started to interact with Frasier, his health had been seriously going downhill. There were times when his mind didn't appear to be working properly. Deacon worried that Frasier hadn't told him everything, certainly might not have shown him everything.

"I haven't seen any yet, but we can look."

Deacon moved to the boxes and began to go through the files. Cece did the same.

"Are you thinking he may have come to the trial to watch?"

"Yes. Killers do that sometimes. As do others who have an interest in how something turns out. If there are photos, we should go over every face present."

There were no photos in the file except the crime scene photos. "We should try the newspaper," Deacon suggested.

"The woman who runs the newspaper, Audrey Anderson, came to see me at the prison last month. She wanted to do an interview." Cece shrugged. "But I said no."

"Maybe you should call her. See what she has. Tell her you're reconsidering her interview."

A smile tugged at her lips. "I was just thinking the same thing."

She used her grandmother's old telephone book to look up the number for the newspaper office and then she made the call. Deacon listened as she played her part, offered to reconsider the interview and then asked for any photos.

"I would really appreciate that." She smiled at Deacon. "When could I pick them up?" She listened for a moment. "Perfect."

When she hung up the phone she said, "She needs

an hour to pull the file. The reporter who covered the case has an entire file of interviews he did and a ton of pictures. She said I could see everything."

"We should put these files away before we go."

She surveyed the scattered pages, then looked at him, startled, as if she had only just realized that someone could break in and steal the files or, worse, burn the house down. After what happened with the electrical box, she certainly should have thought of that.

"We could take them to my place, if you'd like."

"Good idea."

They packed the pages back into the folders and the folders into the boxes. By the time they delivered them to his house, it was time to head to the newspaper office. The *Winchester Gazette* building was one of the oldest in town. It sat just off the courthouse square. As soon as they walked through the door, the receptionist directed them to the conference room on the second floor.

The second floor circled the interior space of the building and opened in the center to the first floor. Glass and steel allowed for near complete transparency of the second floor offices.

Audrey Anderson met them on the landing. Deacon didn't know her but he had seen her face and name on the news and in the paper frequently since his move to Winchester. Audrey Anderson was a mover and a shaker in Franklin County. She knew everyone and made no bones about what she wanted when she went after something.

"Miss Winters." She extended her hand and Cece accepted the gesture and gave her hand a shake.

"This is my friend and neighbor, Deacon Ross."

"Mr. Ross." Anderson gave his hand a firm shake, as well. "It's very nice to see you both. Let's move on to the conference room."

"I appreciate you going to all this trouble," Cece said. "It's very kind of you."

Anderson led the way into the spacious room and gestured to the table in the center. "Thank you for saying so, Cece. May I call you Cece?"

"Of course. Wow." Cece stalled at the table and stared at the mounds of papers and photos.

"I wish I could claim that I was doing this out of the kindness of my heart, but I have a very good but selfish reason for helping you. I want your story."

Cece nodded. "I understand. So you know, I have questions I'd like to find the answers to before I give anyone my story."

"You want the truth."

Cece looked from the other woman to Deacon and back. "Yes."

"Whatever I or my staff can do to help you find it—we are at your disposal." She gestured to the table. "Take your time. Any questions, my office is just down the hall."

Anderson closed the door as she left the room.

"You think she's serious about helping me?" Cece asked.

Deacon glanced toward the office where the woman had disappeared. "I think she recognizes there's a big story here and she wants it. She's a very smart newspaper publisher and she's interested in helping you so she can get an exclusive."

Cece's green eyes filled with emotion. "When I came back, I was certain I wouldn't find anyone who wanted to help me."

More of that guilt heaped onto his shoulders. "Let's get to it."

The photos taken were extensive. There were numerous glossy eight by tens of the courtroom and those present to view the proceedings.

"Take your time," Deacon reminded her. "Point him out if you see him."

He had already spotted a man that matched the description she had given. But there was more than one in overalls and with a beard.

"That's him." She tapped the one he had pegged.

"You're certain?"

She nodded. "One hundred percent."

"Maybe Ms. Anderson can track down his name for us."

"I'll ask her." Cece took the photo and headed to Anderson's office.

Deacon picked up another of the photos. As he surveyed the faces, he stalled on one, his heart stumbling. *Jack*.

His partner sat two rows back from the prosecutor's table. In front of Jack and slightly to his right was Sierra Winters. The photo had captured Jack staring at the young woman.

Deacon grabbed more of the photos and shuffled through them, his heart pounding now.

Two more photos showed Jack in the crowd outside the courthouse, always near Sierra…near enough to reach out and touch her.

Jack was either watching Sierra or the two knew each other.

# Chapter Eleven

The man in the photo was Rayford Prentiss but he no longer lived in the house at the end of Pleasant Ridge Road near Huntland. Audrey Anderson had tracked him down to that address. According to the man who lived there now, Prentiss had not lived there in around seven or eight years.

Convenient.

And frustrating.

Cece wanted to scream. Every time she thought she had found someone or something that might help, it or they turned out to be a dead end.

She glanced at the man behind the wheel. Deacon had been oddly quiet since they left the newspaper. Asking him if something was wrong seemed like the right thing to do but she was nearly afraid to open that door. The way her luck ran, whatever was wrong would likely be a travesty that involved her. For now, she decided to be content in the not knowing.

When he headed across the road from what used to be the Prentiss place, she asked, "Where are we going?"

"To check in with the man's former neighbors.

Maybe some of them knew him and know where he is now."

"Assuming he's still alive," she offered forlornly. The way her luck was running, the man had disappeared without a trace.

"Assuming he's still alive," Deacon agreed.

The laneway to the house on the opposite side of the road was a long one, more than a mile. At the end of that lengthy drive, a farmhouse sadly in need of a fresh coat of paint sat nestled against the side of the mountain, trees crowding in around it. Beyond the thick woods were pastures. They had driven past those on the way here. The yard around the house had been left wooded, adding a layer of privacy most of the farmhouses along this road did not have.

"People who live off the beaten path sometimes answer the door with a shotgun." She'd decided to mention it because Deacon was still fairly new around here. Since he'd spent most of his time in the Nashville area, he might not run into that sort of thing too often. She didn't want him getting shot by some nervous homeowner.

"Do I look like a bad guy?"

Cece couldn't tell if he was kidding or not so she gave him a thorough once-over—the beard-shadowed jaw, the cowboy hat pulled down low on his forehead, well-worn jeans and scuffed cowboy boots.

"I should probably go with you." She reached for the door. "I look a lot more harmless."

He grinned. "All right then."

They climbed out of the truck, met at the hood.

He asked, "You remember any of the folks who live nearby?"

"Maybe if I heard the names I might. But I don't remember any of the houses so far."

She'd never had any reason to be in this neck of the woods. Huntland had its own high school so she hadn't gone to school with any of the people from this area. Not that she recalled, anyway.

"Let's give a knock and see what we find."

As she had predicted, the woman of the house showed up at the door with her shotgun. "You lost? You don't look like those door-to-door Bible thumpers."

"Afternoon, ma'am," Deacon said, his voice and that smile charming as hell.

Cece shivered. Until that moment she hadn't noticed just how deep his voice was. Well, maybe she had noticed, but there was something about the way he said *ma'am* that made her shiver. The smile, well, that was the usual generous one that flowed so easily across his lips.

"My name is Deacon Ross and this is my friend Cece. We're trying to locate my momma's cousin, Rayford Prentiss. We lost contact with him years ago and I wanted to let him know she was real sick and might not be long for this world."

There was something else Cece noticed for the first time. The man could weave a tale way too smoothly. Another shiver went through her, this one for an entirely different reason.

"I think he moved away or died or something. Come

on in and I'll ask Daddy. He'll know. He knows everything about everyone around here."

"I would sure appreciate that, ma'am."

"Geneva Harvey." She lowered the barrel of her weapon, tucked it under her left arm and thrust out her right hand.

Deacon shook her hand and then she offered it to Cece who did the same. Cece was immensely thankful the lady didn't recognize her.

"This way."

Ms. Harvey headed deeper into the house. Deacon closed the door behind them and followed behind Cece. They moved through the living room and then the kitchen. The house smelled of cigarettes and the leftover fried okra sitting in the cast-iron skillet on the stove. Cece could not remember the last time she'd had fried okra. Her grandmother had loved it. Beyond the kitchen was a back hall lined with doors. The bedrooms, she imagined. One of the open doors they passed led to a bathroom, complete with claw-foot tub and vintage pedestal sink, both a little stained.

The woman knocked on one of the closed doors. "Daddy, you decent?"

"Why wouldn't I be? Come on in."

The voice on the other side of the door was rusty and gravelly. When the lady opened the door, cigarette smoked greeted them like a fog rolling in off the lake.

"Daddy, this is Deacon Ross and his friend Cece. They want to know what happened to Mr. Prentiss. You remember him?"

All this she said in a really loud voice. Apparently her daddy was about half deaf.

The man sat in a wheelchair. His bed was the type used in hospitals. His skin was more yellow than white. Even his fingernails were yellow, Cece noted, as he lifted his cigarette to his lips and took a draw.

Beyond the wheelchair and hospital bed, the room looked like most any other. A dresser and a door to what was likely a closet. The windows were raised, and a box fan sat in one, trying its best to draw in the air from outside. Overhead a ceiling fan twirled, dust hanging from its blades like fur lining the collar of a coat.

Next to his chair was a table with a glass and a bottle of Jack Daniels. Now that Cece looked more closely, the man's eyes were bloodshot and rimmed in red.

"Cancer."

Cece started when she realized he was speaking to her. He stared directly at her. Evidently he had noticed her sizing up him and his room.

"I got maybe two months left. The painkillers caused other problems so I decided to handle the discomfort on my own terms."

"I'm sorry." Cancer was not a pleasant way to go.

He laughed, the sound a hoarse throaty sound. "Don't be sorry, little girl. I brought it on myself. Smoked two packs a day my whole life. Drank like a crazy man and basically had a hell of a good time. Dying sucks but it was fun while it lasted."

"Mr. Prentiss, Daddy," his daughter scolded. "They

want to know about the old man who used to live across the road."

"Rayford was more hermit than anything else," he said. "Those last few years he lived across the road he was busy building him one of them bugout places. God only knows where. He was into all that prepping stuff. A little over-the-top, if you ask me."

His daughter made a harrumphing sound. "Like you ain't."

He pointed a glare at her. "I'm not like them crazy ones," he snapped. "Rayford's one of them doomsday preppers. The ones that claim they'll rise up after the rest of us are blown to bits by a nuclear bomb or some such shit."

Cece caught Deacon's gaze. *Resurrection.*

"Do you know how we might find him or his friends?" Deacon asked.

Harvey shook his head. "You don't want no part of that bunch," he warned. "They don't like nobody in their business."

"I just want to see that he gets the news," Deacon assured the man.

Harvey's gaze narrowed. "They don't cotton to outsiders, Mr. Ross. You might as well tell your momma he's a lost cause. 'Course they'll probably be the only ones to survive when we all get poisoned by one of them pharmaceutical companies."

"Some of them still live openly," Cece countered. "They just don't tell anyone about what they do out in the woods."

Harvey nodded. "That's right. But then you have

those who decide to make it a way of life. They sort of vanish. Nobody ever sees them again. They don't want to be seen. They refer to them as the *others*. No one talks about them."

"Thank you, Mr. Harvey," Deacon said. "If you happen to see Mr. Prentiss, let him know I'm looking for him. I bought the old Wilburn place."

Another nod and then Harvey looked directly at Cece. "You're Mason Winters's daughter. The one who killed him."

Cece froze. Not sure what to say. Finally she managed an affirming nod. "I'm his daughter, yes." No use arguing the other with him.

"No offense, but you did the world a favor killing that mean old bastard."

"Daddy," his daughter warned.

"It's okay." Cece managed a half-hearted smile for the other woman. "He's right. My father was a mean old bastard."

Harvey laughed until he lost his breath and started to cough. When he stopped coughing, he looked to Deacon. "I'll send your message, but don't say I didn't warn you."

Deacon thanked him again and Ms. Harvey guided them back to the front door. When they were in the truck and back out on Pleasant Ridge Road headed toward Highway 64, Cece turned to Deacon. "My sister had a boyfriend back then." Cece laughed. "She's actually had a few, according to Levi. But back when the murder happened, there was this one. Her first love, sort of. I think we should talk to him. He was at the house a lot with Sierra. He might be able to tell us anything he heard or saw around the house during that those final few weeks."

"Do you mean the guy who gave your sister an alibi?"

She nodded. "That's the one."

"What's his address?"

"I know where his parents live—where he lived back then."

"Close enough."


SLADE FAIRBANKS HAD BEEN married and divorced twice over the past eight years. He had three kids, none of whom lived with him. He rented a small place in a mobile home park just outside town. His younger sister was only too happy to tell all about her relationship-damaged brother. According to her, Sierra ruined him. He was no good after she was finished with him.

As they drove away, Cece confirmed that she didn't doubt the woman's claims for a minute.

As they neared the address the sister had provided, Deacon asked, "Is that him?"

Cece leaned forward and peered at the man in question. "I think so."

As they pulled into the small driveway she nodded. "Yeah, that's him."

He was attending to something on a small charcoal grill while sucking down a beer. The twenty-something man was shirtless and his jeans hung well below his waist.

Fairbanks stared at them as they climbed out of the

truck. Recognition flared on his face when he realized who Cece was.

"Cece Winters! Well, I'll be damned."

He tossed the spatula he had been using into the chair behind him, threw his apparently empty beer can on the ground and started her way. He hugged her tight, for a good while longer than necessary.

"I heard you were out." He held her at arm's length and looked her up and down. "Damn, girl, you look good for a recently released ex-con."

"Thanks, Slade."

He glanced at Deacon.

"This is my friend, Deacon Ross. We wanted to talk to you for a few minutes if you have the time."

A frown tugged his thick eyebrows together. "What's this about?"

"Sierra."

"Oh, hell." He looked around, wiped his hands on his jeans. "Okay." He grabbed the spatula and shifted two burger patties from the grill to a plate. Then he hitched his head toward the trailer. "Come on in."

As he showed them inside, he talked about how his child support kept him from the lifestyle he had hoped for. "As my daddy says, you make your bed, you gotta lay in it."

Cece asked him about his children. He showed her photos on his phone. Deacon kept quiet and let them do the catching up thing. The man was more likely to talk if he was comfortable and felt as if he were in charge.

"You really do look good, Cece." Fairbanks shook

his head. "I'm glad you got through that time with all that happened. I know it was hard."

"It was. Tough. Especially since I didn't kill anyone, much less my own father."

He looked away then. Stared at the floor.

"Sierra and Marcus said things about me that weren't true," she went on when he didn't look up. "You were close to her back then. Why would she do such a thing?"

His gaze met Cece's and for a half a minute Deacon was certain he intended to balk.

"You know how she was. Selfish, self-centered. She didn't care about anyone but herself."

"What happened to the two of you? You were so good to her."

*Smart move.* Deacon wanted to give her a high five.

"She dumped me like she did all the ones who came after me. You can't satisfy her."

"Was she cheating on you? That seemed to be what she did back then."

·Deacon figured Levi had told Cece that part, as well.

He nodded. "Oh, yeah. She had her an older guy. I caught her with him right before…well, you know. The murder."

Deacon's instincts perked up.

"What old guy?" Cece asked. "I don't remember an old guy."

The fact that she completely passed over his mention of the murder and went straight to the cheating surprised Deacon.

"It was a big secret," Slade said with a heavy dose of derision. "He wasn't from around here. Pretty much no one knew she was involved with him. I found out totally by accident. Walked right up on the two of them in a car, all hugged up."

Deacon's thoughts had gone still at the "he wasn't from around here" part.

"Who was he?" Cece pressed.

Fairbanks shrugged. "I don't know his name. I saw him that once, though. Black hair, a little gray around the temples. I didn't get close enough to see his eyes."

His breath jammed deep in his lungs, Deacon opened the photo app on his cell phone and handed his phone to Cece. She looked at the image on the screen and then showed it to Slade. "Was it this guy?"

He stared for a moment, then his head started to bob up and down. "Yeah, that's him. Creepy old bastard."

Deacon flinched.

"Are you sure they were involved?" Cece asked. "Maybe they were just friends."

He laughed. "No. She bragged about it later. Said he was going to take her away from here. Give her the life she deserved."

"Did they break up? What happened to him?"

Deacon's voice sounded overloud in the room. Cece glanced at him.

Fairbanks stared at him a moment. "I don't know for sure," he said. "I only know that she moved on to somebody else. I never saw the guy again." He turned back to Cece. "You remember Tommy Woosier? She started going with him after that."

Deacon's brain was throbbing. Sierra had been involved with Jack somehow? He stared at Cece. Had he been blaming the wrong sister all along? Deacon lost track of the conversation for the next few minutes as he mulled over the potential facts he'd just had to face.

"I just have one other question, Slade."

Deacon shook off the disturbing thoughts and focused on the conversation between the man and Cece.

"Why did you lie for Sierra that day?"

He paled. "What do you mean? Lie about what?"

"You said you helped Sierra when her car broke down at the time our father was being murdered, but that isn't true because you just said she was cheating on you. You caught her before the murder. The two of you broke up. Why would you help her?"

Holy hell. She was right, Deacon realized. He'd been so stuck on the news about Sierra and Jack, he'd missed that part of the conversation. He couldn't wait to hear the man's answer to that one.

Slade shot to his feet. "Oh, man, you see the time?" He gestured to the clock on the wall. "I have to go. My oldest is expecting me to pick him up."

Cece stood more slowly. Deacon did the same.

"I'm not leaving until you tell me the truth, Slade. I've spent eight years in prison. I deserve to know why."

He held up his hands as if he could stop her words. "I know. I know."

"No, you don't know. You have no idea the things that happened to me in there. Now tell me the truth. You owe me the truth."

"Okay." He nodded about twenty times in five seconds. "But if you say I said it, I'll deny it. That brother of yours—Marcus—told me if I didn't tell the police that story, he would kill me."

Cece stared at Fairbanks, her expression one of utter defeat.

"Now go. I have stuff to do."

The drive back to Cece's place was made in total silence. It wasn't until Deacon parked that he spoke, disrupting the too-quiet space between them.

"You think he's telling the truth?" Deacon asked.

She knew her brother. Knew what he was capable of, even if she hadn't wanted to see it.

"Yes."

"In that case, it looks like Sierra was way deeper into whatever happened than you thought." He twisted in the seat to look at Cece. She stared straight ahead. "Do you think she could have killed your father?"

*Or my partner?* he wanted to say.

"She was a few months from turning sixteen. Just a kid. More important, I never saw her react violently before." She turned to meet his gaze. "But Marcus could have."

"They set you up." The whole damned thing was so crystal clear.

"That's what I've been trying to tell everyone. I didn't know who was setting me up, but I knew for certain that I didn't do it."

Deacon reached to start his truck once more.

"Where are we going?" she asked, her voice suddenly shaking.

"We're going back to see your sister's old boyfriend.

I intend to beat the rest of the truth out of him and then we're calling the sheriff."

That look—the one like a wild animal trapped in the headlights of an oncoming car—claimed her face, filled her eyes. "You believe me?"

Before he could stop himself he grabbed her face in his hands and kissed her. He hadn't meant to. Definitely had not meant to kiss her so hard and so deeply. Her lips felt soft beneath his. Her skin smooth and delicate in his palms. Every cell in his body started to burn. Her fingers touched his hands, trembled, and he wanted to pull her beneath him and do things she would hate him for when this was finished.

When he could control himself once more, he drew his mouth from hers but he could not let go…could not lose that contact. He pressed his forehead to hers. Closed his eyes and reached for reason.

But there was no reason.

Not in this.

# Chapter Twelve

*Tuesday, August 6*

Deacon had spent the night on her couch again.

Cece had wanted him to sleep in her room. Well, sleep wasn't actually what she had wanted. She had wanted more of those hot kisses. She had wanted him to make love to her. Didn't matter that he was basically a stranger. She knew enough. She wanted him. Wanted to know all of him.

But he had talked her out of being in a rush. *There's time*, he had insisted. Time for her to be sure she wasn't making a mistake, he had explained. He had warned that he was a lot older than she was. That he had a history she didn't know and understand. He had even said she shouldn't trust him quite so much.

Then, this morning, he had explained that he had to run an errand and that she should stay in the house, doors locked, shotgun and phone handy.

She had a feeling he was going back to try and locate Slade. He had more questions for him. They hadn't been able to find him again yesterday.

Her mystery seemed to have become extremely important to Deacon. It felt as if he wanted the truth as badly as she did. Warmth spread through her. He cared about her. That was obvious. She didn't fully understand how it was possible given the short time they had known each other. A mere five days ago he had been just the stranger next door—the new neighbor.

But that had all changed now.

At least, for her it had changed.

She rinsed her coffee cup and decided to get back to finding the truth. There had to be something in those files that would help. Deacon had brought them back last night and they'd dug around some more—until it became clear they couldn't be in the same room alone together for another minute. Then she'd gone to bed and he'd crashed on the couch.

As she knelt next to the coffee table and picked up the copies of the photos from the courtroom that Audrey Anderson had provided, she wondered about the man. This K.C. who'd made all those promises to Sierra—at least, according to Slade. Seeing these photos of him certainly made Deacon unsettled. Did he know the man personally? Was that why he'd had to run errands this morning?

There was something…maybe he was right. Maybe she shouldn't trust him so completely.

Knocking at the front door made her jump. Fear slid through her veins. She got to her feet and went for the shotgun in the corner. It was loaded. Deacon had made sure. She moved quietly to the window to peek out to see who her visitor was. She held her breath as she moved aside the shade.

*Sierra.*

Cece scanned the front yard to ensure no one was with her. A car sat in the driveway. Not the same one Levi had driven. She supposed it belonged to her sister. There didn't appear to be anyone else in the vehicle.

Still, she hesitated. Was her little sister capable of murder? Cece just wasn't sure. What if something else had happened? The possibility that Levi had been hurt and Sierra had come to tell her had Cece going to the door and unlocking it. She drew it open, the shotgun in her grasp.

"What do you want?" she demanded.

Sierra looked from Cece to the shotgun and back. "We need to talk."

"Is Levi okay?" Cece resisted the urge to shake her younger sister and demand to know why they couldn't start over and pretend none of this ever happened.

But it had happened.

Sierra had helped to steal Cece's life. God only knew what else she had done.

"I don't know. I haven't seen him. I was hoping you had."

Cece thought of her meeting with Levi at the shack. "No. I haven't seen him."

Sierra closed her eyes. "Oh, God." Her dark eyes suddenly flew open, hatred burning in their opaque depths. "Why did you have to come back? Why didn't you go somewhere else? Anywhere else? There's nothing here for you."

"This is my home as much as it is yours." Though Cece felt anything but at home in this place, she wasn't going to allow her sister to tell her where she belonged or did not belong.

"No one wants you here. Can't you see that? All you do is make everyone restless. Bad things happen when you're here, Cece."

The words hit their mark. All these years Cece had been certain her sister—or anyone else for that matter—could say nothing else to her that would hurt. But she had been wrong.

"Just go, Sierra. Just leave." Cece started closing the door.

Sierra stepped onto the threshold, preventing the door from closing. "I'm warning you, Cece. You should go before something really bad happens."

Cece studied her sister's face, searched her eyes. "Are you high? What kind of drugs are you taking?"

"It doesn't matter," Sierra snapped. "What I do hurts no one but me. I'm trying to help you."

Cece laughed. "You mean, the way you helped me during the trial? You and Marcus practically drove the final nails into my coffin. Why would I believe anything you say now?"

"Believe what you want. But if you're half as smart as you think you are, you'll go before it's too late."

"It's already too late, Sierra. Are you just now seeing that?"

This time her sister stepped back when Cece closed the door.

She locked it, propped the shotgun in the corner and

collapsed against the door. She squeezed her eyes shut and fought back the tears. She had sworn she would never cry over her family again and here she was, blubbering like a fool.

Sierra did not care about her. Marcus sure as hell didn't. God only knew what was on Levi's mind these days. The one thing Sierra had right was that Cece should leave. She did not belong here. She should never have come back.

Except she wanted the truth.

She exhaled a breath. Would it change anything? No. Those eight years were gone. There was no getting them back. Would it prove she wasn't the bad person everyone around here thought she was? Maybe. Maybe not.

Then why didn't she just go? List her grandmother's house with a real estate agency and get the hell on with her life?

Because she could not.

She could not pretend the truth didn't matter.

The truth was all she had.

A knock on the door made her jump away from it.

She gasped. Put a hand to her throat. Damn Sierra. Why didn't she just leave?

Cece unlocked and yanked open the door. "What do you—?"

But it wasn't Sierra standing on her porch now. It was the sheriff.

Fear throttled through her. "What's happened?"

*Please don't let Levi be hurt...or worse.*

"Morning, Miss Winters. You mind if I come in a moment?"

"Of course. Come in, Sheriff Tanner." She considered that the shotgun was in the corner but opted to hope he wouldn't notice. "Sorry. I thought you were someone else."

He smiled as he stepped inside. "I understand. You've had reason to be a little jumpy."

Cece closed the door behind him. "I could make some coffee if you'd like a cup, sheriff. I don't have much else to offer. A glass of water?"

He removed his hat and held it in his hands. "I'm fine. Can we sit and talk for a minute?"

"Of course." She gestured to a chair. "Excuse the mess. I've been going through the files from my court case."

The pages were spread all over the coffee table and some on the couch. She felt confident the gruesome crime scene photos were nothing new to him.

"Your neighbor, Deacon Ross, has been helping you?"

Cece settled onto the couch, knowing the sheriff wouldn't sit until she did. "Yes." She smiled. "He's been very helpful. Kept me out of trouble a couple of times. He's a good neighbor."

The sheriff held her gaze for a long moment before saying more. "I'm afraid I have some potentially troubling information about Mr. Ross."

Fear stabbed deep into Cece all over again. She had been so worried about Levi. Maybe it was Deacon who had been hurt. "Has something happened?"

"Whenever a stranger comes to town and draws our attention in some suspicious way, Chief Brannigan and I try our best to check him out. Make sure the folks we're sworn to protect don't have anything to worry about."

The fear receded but something else, something dark and disturbing swelled inside her. "Is there something I should know about him?"

Tanner nodded. "I'm afraid so. Mr. Ross is an agent with the FBI."

Cece managed a jerky nod. "He told me he worked for the federal government."

A margin of relief trickled through her. Deacon had told her the truth, pretty much. That was good, wasn't it?

"There's more to the story, I'm afraid. I spoke to his superiors again this morning. Mr. Ross has been on a leave of absence for a good while now. Apparently, he took that time off just to come and live here. Next door to you."

She frowned. "I don't understand."

"He bought the Wilburn place because he wanted to be close to where you would be when you came back after your release."

A wave of unsteadiness went through her. "You mean, so he could watch me?"

The sheriff nodded. "Back when your daddy…died, there was a man who went missing. The FBI was all over the county looking for him for a good long while. You won't remember that because you were…"

She nodded. In jail. Awaiting trial. He didn't have to say any of that.

"I didn't recognize Mr. Ross because he was on

some deep cover assignment at the time. But this morning I learned that man who disappeared, Jack Kemp, was his mentor and friend. I believe Mr. Ross has come to Winchester because you're back. He may believe you had something to do with or knew his friend."

Her hand trembling, Cece picked up one of the photos Audrey Anderson had provided and handed it to the sheriff. "Is the man circled in that photo this Jack Kemp?"

Tanner studied the photo then nodded. "That's him." He passed the photo back to Cece. "Did you know him, Miss Winters?"

She shook her head slowly. "But my sister may have."

He stood. "I'm as sorry as I can be that I didn't have this information before now. Under the circumstances, I would be wary of Mr. Ross. I've got my deputies watching for him. When I catch up with him, he and I will have a talk. If you'd prefer, I'll tell him not to bother you anymore."

"He…" Cece stood. Betrayal twisted inside her like barbed wire. But the truth was the truth. "He hasn't bothered me, sheriff. In fact, he probably saved my life the other night. I don't know why he bought the farm next door and I don't know why he befriended me, maybe for the reason you said, but he hasn't done anything to hurt me. He's done exactly the opposite."

Tanner nodded. "All right. I'll still need to talk to him. If you hear from him, you let him know we need to iron out a few things."

She nodded. "When I see him again, I'll tell him."

At the door the sheriff hesitated. "Miss Winters, I wasn't part of the original investigation, but I want you to know that if you would like me to review the case, I'll be more than happy to do so. I'll do whatever I can to help. If you believe justice failed you, I would very much like the opportunity to help make it right. I'm certain Chief Brannigan would be happy to do the same."

Cece barely kept the tears burning in her eyes from sliding down her cheeks. "Thank you so much, sheriff. That means a lot to me."

When he was gone, Cece locked the door and pressed her forehead against the cool wood. All these years she had dreamed of the police realizing their mistake and helping her to find the truth but that had never happened. Then a stranger seemed prepared to do exactly that.

Except she couldn't be certain if he really wanted to help her or if he wanted to link her to whatever happened to his friend.

Either way, he had lied to her. What she'd told the sheriff was true. Deacon had probably saved her life and she appreciated what he had done. But he had used her. She had been used enough in this life. She had been lied to far too many times.

It would be better if she cut her losses where he was concerned.

DEACON WAS ONLY a few miles from Cece's house when blue lights flashed in his rearview mirror. He scrutinized the truck behind him.

Colt Tanner. The Franklin County sheriff.

Deacon slowed and eased to the side of the road, put his truck in Park and powered down his window. He watched as Tanner climbed out of his own truck, set his hat into place and then strode toward Deacon's door.

"Sheriff." He gave the other man a nod. "Was I speeding?"

Deacon doubted the sheriff had pulled him over for the five miles per hour over the posted speed limit he had been going. This was about something else. He wouldn't need three guesses to hit the right one. Tanner had been making calls. Deacon had gotten a heads-up from one of his colleagues.

"We need to talk, Ross. Can you follow me back to my office?"

Deacon assessed the man. "Any reason we can't talk right here?"

Tanner glanced up and then down the road. "I guess not. Mind if I join you?"

"Make yourself at home." Deacon pressed the button to unlock the doors.

The sheriff walked around the back of the truck and climbed into the passenger seat. He sat for a moment before he said anything. Deacon recognized the strategy. He hoped to escalate the tension. No need. Deacon's tension was already sky-high and it had nothing to do with the man seated across the console from him.

"I don't think you've been completely up-front with me, Mr. Ross."

"Deacon," he corrected. "You should call me Deacon."

"Well, Deacon, I spoke to your supervisor up in Nashville and he seemed to think you might be on a mission down here—one that has nothing to do with purchasing less expensive property or helping out a new friend."

"You could say my mission here is twofold," Deacon admitted. "When I first came, it was for a singular purpose, but I realized I liked the area so I decided to buy land." He was wasting his time. The man knew why he was here, but that didn't mean Deacon had no choice but to spill his guts.

"I don't have a problem with a fellow lawman looking for the truth." Tanner shrugged. "Hell, if I thought a case hadn't been investigated properly or that stones had been left unturned, I would be all over it. Particularly if that case carried some personal significance for me."

"Jack Kemp was a good friend," Deacon said, deciding to play this a different way. "He trained me. There wasn't a better man in the Bureau. All I want is to know what happened to him."

"He disappeared around the same time Mason Winters was killed?"

Deacon nodded. "He was here investigating the group that calls themselves Resurrection. They're vastly different from the usual prepper folks. They're extremists with fanatical views. Jack was part of a joint task force with the ATF. I can't go into all the details because I don't know everything there is to know, but there was speculation that this doomsday prepper group was working with others across the country."

"Running guns," Tanner guessed.

"Among other things," Deacon allowed. "These people live in communities. They go the extra mile not to stand out, to blend in. No one knows who they are. They're careful and very hard to catch. Their one goal is to ensure the success of their mission."

"Their mission is?" Tanner asked.

"To be prepared to resurrect mankind when the rest of us destroy ourselves."

Tanner grunted. "Interesting. Your friend was attempting to infiltrate this group?"

Deacon nodded. "More than two decades ago, Jack lived here for months in hopes of finding a way into the group that had just started in your county. The belief is that he thought the church Mason Winters had started was connected. When the case went cold, Jack was reassigned. Nine years ago, he came back for a follow-up. He was here a few weeks and then he disappeared. I need to know what happened to him."

"You could have come to me," Tanner argued. "It's important to me that the residents of my county are safe. If this Resurrection group represents some threat, I'd like to know."

"That's the problem," Deacon said. "You could be one of them."

Tanner's face showed his unhappiness with that comment. "I'm not."

Deacon held up his hands. "I'm not accusing you,

sheriff. I'm merely pointing out the dilemma involved with this kind of investigation."

"According to your boss," Tanner countered, "there is no investigation. The one your friend was a part of was closed years ago. Mr. Kemp was declared legally dead last year."

"There's no official investigation," Deacon admitted. He wasn't going to play games with the sheriff. "But I'm not finished yet."

After an extended stare down, Tanner nodded. "All right. I'm good with that as long as you keep me informed and don't do one damned thing that breaks the law."

Deacon nodded his agreement. "I can live with that."

"What do you believe happened to your friend?"

"My guess is, he got caught and he's buried around here somewhere. But he has a wife and a family who need closure. I want to find that for them."

Tanner considered his answer for a moment. "I got the impression your people don't want you stirring this particular pot."

"The joint task force doesn't exist anymore. The Bureau backed off and turned the investigation over to the ATF. Politics. Someone somewhere wanted to do things a different way and that was that."

"But you can't walk away?"

"It took me years to find out where he was assigned and what he had been doing. I still don't know all the details, but I know he was here. And then he disappeared."

"But you found him in those courtroom photos of the Winters murder case."

Deacon confirmed his assessment with a nod, not that the sheriff needed his confirmation. He already knew the answers.

"Like I said, I'll be happy to work with you, Ross. See if we can figure out what happened to your friend. But you need to leave Cece Winters out of this. She's been through enough. She doesn't need you using her. She's been let down by everyone around her—except maybe her grandmother. She spent nearly nine years in jail and in prison. She came back here looking for the truth. She sees you as some sort of hero. If you can't be that hero, you need to leave her be."

"I'll talk to her," Deacon promised. He should have already. "Explain myself."

"Just so you know," Tanner explained, "I've already talked to her. She knows why you're here." He reached for the door. "I expect you to handle this properly. You have an obligation to protect and serve the same as I do. When you're ready, we'll talk strategy for this investigation of yours. I mean what I say, don't forget that."

He got out and walked back to his truck. Deacon waited until he had driven away before he did the same.

At Cece's driveway, he made the necessary turn. He parked near the house and climbed out. When this thing started, he'd anticipated telling her the truth. He had intended to come in, find what he needed and ensure she paid for the crime if she was responsible in any way for what happened to Jack. And then he would be gone.

Except nothing had worked out the way he planned. She wasn't the person he had thought she was.

Cecelia Winters wasn't a killer.

Like Tanner said, she had been let down by everyone she had counted on and she deserved better than what Deacon had given so far.

She opened the door before he knocked. She stared at him, the hurt in her eyes a punch to the gut.

"Did you have more lies you wanted to tell me?"

He removed his hat. "No. I've told you too many already."

Before he could apologize, she held up her hand. "Don't. I don't want to hear anything else you have to say. I appreciate that in some ways you've helped me. I truly do. But you came here to use me. I can't get past that." She shook her head. "Did you think I killed my father and your friend? What kind of person do you think I am?"

"I didn't come here to use you or to prove you..." He closed his eyes a moment. "I don't know. Maybe I did. But I was wrong."

"Why? Because you got caught? Would you have told me the truth if the sheriff hadn't told me first?"

"I want the truth, Cece. Just like you. I didn't come for anything else. Just the truth. I wasn't expecting things to become personal. But they did, and as sorry as I am for misleading you, I'm not sorry about anything else."

She looked away. "I wish I could believe you."

"I can't make you believe me, but I can urge you to let me help you with this. We're close. I know it and I think you do, too. Let me help you. You can trust me. You have my word."

"Your word isn't worth much, Mr. Ross. I started

this alone and I'm pretty sure that's how it'll end. I'm not counting on anyone. Not anymore. You would think I'd learned that years ago but I still allowed you to lead me down that path. Don't expect me to be grateful you feel bad about it now. Goodbye, Deacon."

She closed the door.

He knocked hard. "Cece, please let me help you."

She didn't answer.

He flatted his hands against the slab of wood that stood between them and leaned his face there. "You shouldn't do this alone."

"I've always been alone."

The key turned in the lock and he didn't need X-ray vision to know she had moved away from the door.

He had screwed up and he wasn't sure he could fix it.

## Chapter Thirteen

Cece washed her face, then stared at her reflection in the mirror. How had she allowed Deacon to fool her so thoroughly? Had she not learned anything?

Eight years in a damned prison should have taught her something besides how to be beaten and threatened and terrified.

Look at Levi. She had sincerely believed he was on her side and look what he had done. Even if there were moments when she thought differently—like Deacon saving her from Ricky—everyone she had counted on proved her a fool in the end.

"What the hell is wrong with you?"

She turned away from her reflection and went back to the living room. She checked out the window to make sure he was gone.

The yard was empty. The driveway was deserted.

She was alone again.

She shouldn't have expected anything different, yet she had allowed herself to hope. That kiss…that one damned kiss…shouldn't have made her dream of the possibility, but it had. She had dared to believe.

Damn it.

In the living room she stared at the stack of papers and photos. She should take the whole pile out back and burn it. She should list the house and walk away. Never look back. Never, ever come back.

Sierra hated her. Marcus hated her.

Who knew what Levi was doing or thinking. Whatever was on his mind, it wasn't being there for her.

Why waste any more time? She was nearly thirty years old. There was the college fund. She had a chance at a real life.

Except the past would haunt her forever. She had realized this already. Pretending it wasn't so wouldn't change a damned thing.

A murder charge did not just go away.

She had to see this through. Either she would do it alone or she would take the sheriff up on his offer. She didn't really know Colt Tanner but he seemed sincere.

Then again, so had Deacon Ross.

The fact was that she just could not trust her instincts anymore. Apparently, she never could.

The phone rang, the trill echoing through the house. She jumped. If it was Deacon she was hanging up on him.

She picked up the receiver. "Hello."

"Cece?"

"Levi? Where are you? Are you okay?"

"I… I need you to come to the house. Marcus wants to talk to all of us."

Levi's voice sounded strange. Something was very wrong. "Are you all right, Levi?"

"Can…" He cleared his throat. "Can you come?"

"Of course. I'll be right there. I just need to know that you're okay."

When he didn't say anything else, she said, "Levi? Did you hear me? I'm coming."

Worried, she started to hang up but shouting stopped her. She pressed the receiver back to her ear.

"Don't come, Cece! Don't come! It's a trap!"

The line went dead.

Fear and fury exploded inside her. Damn Marcus. She'd had enough.

She stormed across the room, grabbed her shotgun and headed for the truck. She wasn't playing with him anymore.

Outside, she strode to the barn, opened the doors and climbed into the truck. She propped the gun against the seat next to her and took off. She didn't bother getting out to close the barn doors the way her grandmother had taught her. She didn't care anymore. Levi was in trouble and she intended to find out what the hell was going on.

The drive to the house where she had grown up only took fifteen minutes but that was fifteen minutes too long. There were no other vehicles in the driveway. No guards strolling around.

Maybe she should have gone to the church.

She got out, reached back in for her shotgun and walked toward the front door. Someone had to be here. If her grandmother's phone hadn't been so old she would have had caller ID and maybe she would have known for sure where the call came from. Guess it wouldn't have mattered since it was probably a cell phone. Everybody had them.

Except her.

She banged on the door. It flew inward. Since no one was standing there she figured it must have been ajar. Listening for the slightest sound, she stepped across the threshold. The house was as silent as a tomb. Goose bumps raised on her flesh.

"Levi?"

His name echoed in the silence.

Cece took a deep breath and moved beyond the entry hall and into the living room. The room was a mess. Books pulled off shelves and slung across the floor. Couch and chair cushions yanked out of place.

What the hell happened here?

Her heart bumped into a faster rhythm. "Sierra?"

No response. Nothing but her voice reverberating in the deafening silence. She moved on to the dining room. Broken dishes that had once been in the china cabinet were scattered over the wood floor. Chairs were upside down and silverware had been tossed out of drawers.

"Marcus?"

She walked through the kitchen that was in the same condition and prepared to take the three steps down to the family room her father had added on when they were kids.

Marcus stood on the other side of the room, one hand resting on the mantel of the fireplace. Sierra sat on the couch. Neither turned to look at Cece.

"Where's Levi?"

Sierra said nothing. Just sat there and stared as if she were in a coma.

"Marcus," Cece demanded, "where is Levi?"

"He's gone."

Still, he didn't look at her.

"What do you mean he's gone? He just called me and said I needed to come here."

"He made a mistake, Cece. The same way you did." Marcus turned to her finally. He moved toward her and Sierra started to sob.

"What're you talking about? I know what I did. I stood up to that bastard. What did Levi do?"

"He turned against us. Against our family. The same way you did."

He kept coming. Cece tightened her grip on the shotgun.

"This family turned against me." She spat the words at him. "Have you turned on Levi now?"

"Family is all that matters. If we don't stick together, we're nothing."

Cece aimed the shotgun at his chest. "Where is he?"

"You should have stayed gone, Cece. We were fine. We had moved on. But you had to come back and stir it all up again."

"Stop right there," she warned. "Where is Levi?"

"He's gone," Marcus said again, his dark eyes boring into her like hot coals. "It was the only way to save him."

"What does that mean?" Rage roared through her. He was just like their father. Heartless and self-centered. Insane.

"But you—you can't just go. You keep coming back. We can't have that anymore, Cece. This has to be finished once and for all."

"You're just like our father," she accused. "Evil and full of yourself. You think you're God. Just like he did. You don't get to decide who goes and who lives or dies. Did you kill him? To take all the power for yourself? Is that what happened, Marcus? Did you stab our father for all the times he made you feel so small and insignificant?"

"Goodbye, Cece."

She shook her head and steadied the shotgun. "I'm not going anywhere. Not until you tell me what you've done with Levi."

The blow to her head came from behind her. She pitched to the floor like a rag doll tossed aside. The shotgun landed a few feet in front of her. She saw it lying there. Told herself to reach for it, but her body wouldn't respond.

Feet moved into her line of vision. Small, bare feet. A face was suddenly in front of hers.

*Sierra*.

"You should have listened to me, Cece. Now it's too late."

DEACON RODE OUT another hit.

Ricky Olson grinned. "Don't that feel good, buddy? Our time together was cut short the other night. I thought we would finish up tonight. Then I'm going over there and picking up where I left off with Cece."

Olson's two thugs had Deacon's arms pulled behind

his back. In order to hold him the way their buddy had instructed, they'd had to put their weapons away. Olson, on the other hand, still had his in one hand.

Deacon stretched his neck. Licked his bloody lip. "Is that all you've got, Olson? I can see why Cece wasn't satisfied."

The snorts from the guys behind him helped Deacon out more than they would ever know. Fury claimed Olson's face. He jammed his nine millimeter into his waistband and prepared to throw his full attention and weight into his next punch.

That was Deacon's cue. With his right arm, he flung the guy clamped around it toward Olson. Then he grabbed the one on his left with his newly freed right hand and twisted his head hard enough to nearly break his neck. When the guy jerked away, Deacon snagged his weapon.

He put the barrel in Olson's face just as he lunged for him. "Come on," Deacon urged. "Draw your weapon. Flinch. Something. So I can shoot your sorry butt."

Olson froze. Both his buddies did, too.

"On the floor," Deacon ordered. "Facedown."

When the three were nose down on the hardwood, Deacon took their belts and secured their hands behind their backs. He claimed their weapons as his own. He ripped off the first guy's sneakers and used his tube socks to secure his feet. Then he did the same to the other two. All three cursed and threatened the whole time. Deacon ignored them.

"Nice to see you again, gentlemen. I'll let the sheriff know you're here waiting for pickup."

Deacon rushed out the door. He had been watching Cece's house and saw her heading out to the barn in a hurry. She'd had her shotgun with her. He had rushed back to his place to get his truck and been met by Olson and his welcoming party.

He climbed behind the wheel of his truck and started the engine. Just in case the three got loose before he expected, he drove around their truck and fired a round into each tire. That should keep them here for a while.

As he drove down the road, he tossed their weapons into the ditch one by one. He pulled into Cece's driveway and barreled toward the house. The doors where the truck was usually parked stood open. He climbed out, rushed up the front steps and knocked on the door. When she didn't answer, he gave the knob a twist. The door opened. He scanned the living room. The phone receiver dangled from its curly cord instead of resting on the base. He walked into the kitchen. The back door stood wide open. Wherever she had gone, she had been upset and it had something to do with a phone call.

Had to be Levi or Sierra. Maybe Marcus.

He bounded out to his truck and drove to the church since he passed its location first. The building and the parking area were empty so he drove to Marcus's house next.

Cece's truck wasn't in the driveway.

Damn it.

When he would have backed away, someone peeked out the window. The curtain fell just as quickly as it had moved aside.

His instincts started to hum. Maybe it was nothing.

But there was no one else in this town who would go to the trouble to find Cece's new number and call her. She had no friends.

He shut off the engine and got out. He tucked his weapon at the small of his back and then closed the truck door. Listening for the slightest sound and scanning from left to right and back, he walked toward the front door.

It opened before he raised his hand to knock.

"Can I help you?"

Marcus Winters.

"I hope so." Deacon relaxed into the part of friendly neighbor. "I'm looking for Cece. She mentioned she was coming by to see Levi. Is she here?"

Marcus shook his head. "I haven't seen or heard from her in years. I hope I never do."

Deacon hummed a note of confusion. "That's strange. She said she spoke to you on the phone just a little while ago."

Something flashed in Marcus's eyes before he could conceal it. Oh, yeah. He had seen her.

"As you can see," he gestured to the driveway and yard behind Deacon, "her truck isn't here. Obviously she is not here."

"Maybe I should talk to Levi. Is he here?"

"He is not."

"Well, I suppose I can talk to Sierra. She's here. I saw her in the window."

The statement wasn't entirely true, but unless she actually wasn't here, this asshole couldn't know that.

"Very well." Marcus turned away from the door

and walked to the bottom of the staircase. He shouted for his younger sister. Eventually Sierra came down the stairs.

"This man wants to talk to you." Marcus walked on into the house, leaving the two of them alone.

For a moment Deacon could not speak. This woman had been involved somehow with Jack. She could very well know what happened to him.

Focus. He was here about Cece.

"I was looking for Cece. She said she was coming here. Have you seen her?"

Sierra shook her head. "No. Haven't talked to her either."

She was lying. The woman was as transparent as glass. Deacon resisted the impulse to grab her and shake the hell out of her.

"Thanks for your time. I guess I misunderstood."

Deacon turned and started toward the door.

The shotgun propped against the wall next to the door stopped him.

He saw the carved heart on the stock.

Cece's shotgun.

Rather than confront the two, he walked on out the door. Whatever had happened, he was going to need help.

He climbed into his truck, turned around and drove off. Once he was on the road, he found a place to back into the edge of the woods and pulled out his cell. He called the sheriff's department and waited while the dispatcher patched him through to Tanner. Before Deacon had finished filling him in, Tanner had already ordered a unit to Cece's house just in case she showed up there. He assured Deacon he would join him ASAP.

"You should probably send a unit to my house," Deacon said as an afterthought. "I left Ricky Olson and his two pals tied up on the floor. I'll explain when I see you."

Deacon ended the call and focused on the driveway that led back to the Winters' home place.

The next eight or ten minutes were some of the longest in his life. Tanner pulled in and parked directly in front of Deacon's truck. The road was so narrow there wasn't room to park beside him.

Deacon met him between the two trucks and briefed him. "No one has gone in or come out. Unless there's another entrance onto the property."

"I'm pretty sure that's the only one," Tanner said. He searched Deacon's face for a moment. "You're certain about the shotgun?"

"Positive. It belonged to her grandmother. Look, Tanner, I don't want to waste time. The bastard knows where she is. He's holding her hostage or—"

"I'm going over there to talk to him."

Deacon wanted to argue but the man was right. "Do what you have to."

"Stay put," Tanner warned.

Deacon nodded. He knew the drill. But that didn't mean he liked it.

He watched Tanner back out onto the road and head down the driveway across the road. He paced the length of his truck about a hundred times before Tanner came back. He parked, climbed out, shook his head.

"Damn it." Deacon knew Marcus and Sierra were lying.

"The shotgun wasn't by the front door anymore."

"I'm telling you it was there."

Tanner considered the situation a moment. "I know this family was torn apart by the father's death. Sides were taken. Seems like the whole bunch, except maybe Levi, turned on Cece, believed her guilty. But do you really believe Marcus or Sierra would do anything to hurt her? Physically, I mean?"

"Absolutely. Marcus Winters is a fanatic. You have to know that. Even Cece believes her sister is on drugs. Levi suddenly goes missing. Now Cece. Look, sheriff, you gave me this whole lecture about how she had been let down by everyone around her. Well, whatever you think of me, don't let her down because you don't trust me."

"All right. But we have to do this right. I'll get a search warrant for the shotgun. That'll give us legal cause to search the property."

"How long will that take?" Deacon did not intend to stand around here and wait.

"I know a judge. It shouldn't take long. A couple of hours."

Deacon shook his head. "No way am I waiting that long."

"No problem," Tanner said, his own anger tinging his words. "I can arrest you."

Deacon held up his hands. "How about I go into the woods over there and watch the property? I won't go near the house. I won't make a damned sound."

"Don't you approach that house, Ross. Don't you do a damned thing until you hear from me."

"Unless I see Cece, you have my word."

"Fair enough."

Tanner got back into his truck and drove away. Deacon ensured the road was clear and then he ducked into the woods. He moved carefully, watching, listening, until he reached a spot where he could see both the front and the rear entrances of the home. He ensured his cell phone was on vibrate and then he watched.

Whatever the cost, he was not going to let Cece down.

## Chapter Fourteen

When Cece's eyes opened it was dark. She rolled onto her side. Her skull protested, the ache deep in her head threatening to expand. Somehow she forced herself to sit up. It was so dark.

Had she been unconscious that long? It had been early afternoon when she went to the house demanding to see Levi.

Sierra had hit her. Not Marcus.

Cece gingerly touched the back of her head. Why would Sierra protect Marcus?

They had ganged up on Cece during the trial and they were still doing it. Did they really believe she killed their father?

Is that why they hated her so?

Even if she had killed him—which she had not— why would they turn on her with such total aversion? Their father had been cruel and unforgiving. He had been particularly hard on Marcus. Marcus should have hated him more than anyone else.

Maybe he had.

Cece sat in the darkness, her head throbbing, and

thought of all she had seen since her return five days ago. Marcus was in control. The church was his now, their father's followers were his followers. The family farm was his, too. And Sierra was his faithful disciple. When it came to motives, Marcus's had not been particularly clear eight years ago. He had been a loving son, one who only wanted his father's approval no matter how hurtful the man was to him.

Cece almost laughed. None of them had ever come close to having the bastard's approval.

She pushed aside the thought. But Marcus's motive was clear now. He was all-powerful now. He had everything.

It was him.

Cece crawled until she found what felt like a wall and she used it to lever herself upright. Slowly, she moved along that wall. Within a few feet, maybe six or eight, she hit a corner and another wall. She repeated this process until she had traced all four walls and discovered the door.

The door was locked. Did not move or rattle when she pushed against it with her entire body weight. There were no windows and the walls felt like stone.

Her head still aching, she closed her eyes and tuned out all thought. She focused on what she smelled. Dank. Musty.

*Earth.*

She lowered to her hands and knees again and felt the floor. Stone, she decided.

*A basement.*

There was a basement in their childhood home.

That must be where they were holding her. Though she didn't remember a small, lockable room. Marcus could have built one. She squeezed her eyes shut and forced her mind to go back in time. She and Levi had played in the basement sometimes.

*Brick.*

The floors and walls had been brick. Not stone.

Maybe Marcus had had another room dug and used stone in it. She climbed back to her feet and moved to the door once more. She felt her way all around the perimeter, following the seam between it and the jamb. The knob wouldn't budge. She tried pushing again. No luck.

"Think, Cece."

She extended her arms and walked through the center of the room, using her arms as if she were doing a breast stroke to ensure she didn't run into anything.

Light suddenly filled the room. She closed her eyes against the brightness. Then blinked and looked around. Fluorescent lights overhead glared down at her.

The scrape of metal against metal warned someone was at the door.

Cece spun around.

The door swung inward.

*Sierra.*

Instinctively Cece stepped back.

Her sister wrung her hands in front of her, the chain of keys clinking as she did so. "I'm sorry I had to hit you, Cece. I was afraid of what he was going to do so I did something first."

Cece scrubbed her palms against her legs, felt the

grit and dirt on her jeans from where she had crawled around on the stone floor. And it was stone. Floor, walls, ceiling. She could see that now.

"Why?" She decided to start there. "What did I do to make the two of you hate me so much?"

Sierra shook her head. "I've never hated you. It was Marcus. He's the one who wanted you to go away forever. He thought that would happen when you were blamed for the murder. But it didn't. You came back and he doesn't want you here."

Cece shook her head. "I don't understand. Why did he want me gone so badly?"

Not once in her life could Cece remember being mean to her brother. He was six years older. Maybe being the only child for so many years had made him resent her. He had never said anything. And what made her different from Levi or Sierra? They had prevented him from being an only child, as well.

Sierra leaned against the wall as if she were too tired to remain standing without assistance. "I don't know. But he wants you gone and this time I think he has something awful planned."

Cece ignored the way her heart started to pound, the way the fight-or-flight instinct roared inside her. "Where is Levi?"

Dear God, what if he had already harmed Levi?

Sierra shook her head. "I don't know. He left. He said he had something to do. He wouldn't tell me what. I think it had something to do with you or that man who moved into the Wilburn place."

"Deacon? Why would Levi have a problem with

Deacon Ross?" Cece thought of Deacon's partner, Jack Kemp. She also thought of the photos of Kemp with Sierra sitting so near him.

How could all this insanity have happened with her so oblivious? School. Work. She had been pretty busy. She had been finishing up her senior year of high school and working every possible shift at the diner. Since she was living with her grandmother, she had been really out of touch with what was going on at home. Basically she had abandoned Levi and Sierra. But she had not wanted to. Her father had kicked her out. She'd had no choice.

"Did you know a man who went by the name K.C.? Dark hair and eyes." Like you, Cece realized. Sierra had those same dark eyes and the dark hair, far darker than that of their father and brothers.

Sierra looked startled. "He…he came around a few times. He said he knew Mom a long time ago. But they lost touch."

The idea of what that could mean—that Sierra was the only one in the family with that dark hair and those dark eyes—slammed into Cece. Levi and Marcus had hair that was brown with the slightest red highlights. A sort of cross between their mom and their dad. But Sierra, she was nothing like any of them.

Was it possible this K.C.—this Jack Kemp—was her biological father?

Wait, wait, wait. That did not make sense. Obviously the blow to her head had done far more damage than Cece realized. Her mother wouldn't have cheated on their father…would she? He *had* been a cruel and hurtful man.

Sierra blinked. "But no." She shook her head adamantly. "I didn't really know him."

She was lying. Cece could see it in her eyes. The eyes that did not belong to a daughter of Mason Winters.

"Tell me the truth, Sierra. That's the only way any of us are going to get through this."

Sierra stared at her for a long moment, her gaze bleary like an inebriated person's.

"What kind of drugs are you taking?" Cece asked.

"I'm not doing anything wrong," Sierra shouted. "I take what the doctor prescribes. For my anxiety and depression."

Cece nodded. "I see. I didn't know."

"Of course you didn't know. You've been gone. Far longer than eight years. You don't know the things he did to me."

"Do you mean the man, K.C.?"

"No!" That she shouted the word warned she did not want to talk about this mysterious man.

"Tell me, please." Cece moved closer to her. "I'm your sister. I want to know."

"He started doing things to me when I was twelve."

Cece could not speak. That would have been the year after their father kicked her out. "You mean, sexually?"

Sierra looked away. "Yes."

"Oh, my God." She started to demand why Sierra

hadn't told anyone but she stopped herself. Of course she hadn't told anyone. She was ashamed and afraid.

"That day. The day he died. I told him I knew the truth. I knew he wasn't my father. I was going to the police. I decided I didn't care what people said or thought when the truth came out. I was going to make sure he paid. My real father had promised to take me away from here. He realized the first time he saw me that I was his daughter. The bastard took that from me."

Cece put her hand against the wall, her knees suddenly weak. "What did he do?"

"He laughed and said our mother was a whore and that if the devil who fathered me really wanted me he would have come back for me a long time ago."

"K.C.?" Cece's voice sounded hollow.

"His name was Jack. Jack Kemp. He was going to take me away from here. He had come to Winchester on some sort of assignment or mission but he said he didn't care about that. He had to get me away from the bastard raping me."

"What did you do when Mason said these things to you?"

"I told him I was going to find Jack and that I was leaving. I ran into the kitchen and grabbed his truck keys but he caught me before I could get out the back door. We struggled. The knife was in the drainer with the other dishes I had washed that morning." She stared at the floor. "I stabbed him."

Cece swallowed back the bitter taste of bile. "You had no choice."

"He staggered back and I kept stabbing him. Over and over and over."

"You didn't call for help?"

Sierra shook her head, the slightest movement. "I was going to, but Marcus came in. He said I would go to prison. That no one would believe the things he had been doing to me. Everyone always thought Daddy and I were so close. He said they would think I was a monster."

Cece forced air into her lungs. "That's when you decided to blame me."

Sierra's gaze collided with hers. "Marcus made me say it. He said if I didn't do what he said, he would make sure everyone knew the truth about me and that he would tell people how I planned the murder and…" She closed her eyes and shook her head. "He said you deserved whatever happened to you for deserting us. You never cared about anyone but yourself. He said because of all the public fights you and Daddy had that people would believe you killed him. He said you would get off on a self-defense plea, anyway. By the time I knew that wasn't going to happen, it was too late to change my story."

Cece swiped at a damned tear that rolled down her cheek. "I guess Marcus told you that, too."

"He said they would know I had planned the whole thing then. I would get the death penalty."

"You were fifteen years old, Sierra. You wouldn't have gotten the death penalty. You probably wouldn't have even gone to prison."

Tears poured down Sierra's cheeks. "I didn't know. I

just did whatever Marcus told me to do. When he came in and saw what I had done, he made me swear never to tell a soul. He said everything would be fine. I just had to be quiet for a little while."

"Did you tell Jack?"

She shook her head. "Marcus said I could never tell anyone, so I didn't. Not until now."

"What happened to Jack?"

She shrugged. "I saw him at the trial a couple of times and he kept asking me questions about what happened. About you and everything…and then he just disappeared."

Cece felt ice slip through her veins. "Did you tell anyone about Jack asking you all those questions?"

"I told Marcus. I was afraid not to."

Dear God, what had her brother done? No more talking. They needed to get out of here. "Sierra—"

"I know what you're thinking," her sister said, cutting Cece off. "You're thinking Marcus killed Jack."

Cece had a bad feeling that was the case. "Is that what you think happened?"

She shrugged. "I don't know. Marcus has taken care of me all this time. He makes sure I'm okay."

"Did he take you to the doctor who gave you the medicine?"

Sierra nodded. "He's been a good brother to me." She looked to Cece then. "But what he did to you— what I did to you—was wrong. We have to fix that now."

"We should go for help," Cece urged. She took Sierra by the arm. "Sheriff Tanner can help us."

Deacon, too, she wanted to say, but she wasn't sure where she stood with him. He had misled her and she wasn't certain she could forgive him for lying to her.

"You go," Sierra said. "I'll stay here and take care of Marcus. He needs me. He doesn't have anyone else."

"Sierra." Cece took her by the shoulders and shook her a little. "We both have to go. We don't know what Marcus might do. He isn't well." A man who would do the things he had done couldn't be well. The sort of help he needed wasn't anything Sierra could give him.

"He's too close," Sierra argued. "We can't get away. If I distract him, you can."

Well, hell. "We'll figure something out," Cece argued. "I'm not leaving without you and then we have to find Levi."

She hoped Marcus had not hurt Levi.

"There's no way out," Sierra insisted.

"Wait." Cece held up her hands. "Explain to me where we are." She glanced around the room. "This doesn't look familiar to me."

"Marcus and some of the followers built a tunnel between the house and the church. There are rooms down here and…and things stored."

*Things?* There was no time for Cece to pursue the idea of what other things might be stored down here. She had been right; this was a basement of sorts. "Where was Marcus when you came down here?"

"He's at the church with his elders. They're discussing what to do." She lifted her gaze to Cece's. "With you."

"Then we'll go back toward the house." Cece ushered Sierra out of the cell-like room. "Which way?"

Sierra stalled. "If they find us, they'll give us to the *others*. No one comes back from the *others*."

"What's the *others*?"

"A place where you learn lessons you never forget."

Cece whirled around at the voice. *Marcus*. Thankfully he was alone.

"We just want to leave, Marcus," Cece informed him. "We don't want to be here."

"Do you want her to tell them what you did?" Marcus asked Sierra.

"She protected herself," Cece countered. "Protecting herself isn't against the law."

"Even if she killed a man in the process?" Marcus glared at her, his brown eyes glowing with anger.

"He was hurting her. You knew this," Cece accused him. "You let her believe she had done something wrong and you knew better."

He laughed. "You deserved what you got. More than you got," he sneered. "You should have died in that prison. Old and withered. You don't deserve a life."

Cece scooted Sierra behind her. She wasn't sure if her brother had a weapon or not but she wasn't taking any chances. "What did I ever do to you, Marcus? You turned on me for no reason."

He laughed even louder then, the sound filled with sheer hatred. "You honestly don't remember, do you?"

"I don't know what you're talking about." She eased back a step, ushering Sierra along with her. "What is it you think I did?"

"You found the hole I made in your wall."

What the hell was he talking about? "What hole?"

"The one I made so I could watch you. The same kind I made in the wall to Sierra's bedroom."

The memory of catching her brother touching himself while staring through a tiny hole in the wall rushed into her mind, pressed the breath from her lungs. "You mean, when you were watching Sierra take a bath? My God, that was when I was, what? Seven? Eight? I didn't even remember until you mentioned it just now."

"You were seven. I was thirteen."

"We were kids," Cece argued. "Young boys do stuff like that. Trade porn magazines and sneak peeks at any girl available—including sisters. It's hormones."

"Do you know what our father did to me?"

She didn't recall any particular punishment. "Did he beat you?" She vaguely remembered Marcus being ill. Had he been in the hospital, too? "I'm so sorry, Marcus. I was a child. I didn't mean to get you into trouble—"

"He and three of his followers said it was necessary to exorcise the lust from me. They kept me in a sweat room, beat me, prayed over me. For days they attempted to rid me of the evil they claimed had possessed me. Then they tested me."

Cece was terrified of what he meant by the last. "Tested you how?"

"They showed me photos of naked girls. When I grew aroused, they announced I had failed the test."

"Oh, my God. I didn't know."

More of that cruel laughter. "That was when they decided that extreme measures had to be taken."

What they'd already done wasn't extreme enough? "Marcus, you know he was evil. He was a sick bastard who damaged us all."

Marcus shook his head. "They castrated me. He said because I lusted after my own sisters I wasn't worthy of being a whole man. They had to cut out the wicked part of me. So they removed my testicles. All because you told him what you saw while I was still too young to fight him."

Dear God. No wonder her brother hated her. "He was the one who was evil, Marcus. Look what he did to Sierra. He threw me out when I was still a kid. He was the devil. He was the evil one."

"You were the lucky one, Cece," Marcus argued. "The one who looked like our whore mother. He couldn't stand it, couldn't bear to look at you. I remember the night he killed her. He pushed her down those stairs and let her lay there and die. He had realized that Sierra wasn't his child. He tortured her until she confessed and then he threw her down the stairs like a piece of trash. When I tried to call for help, he locked me in the basement. You see, Cece, you got away scot-free. You were the lucky one. How can you complain about a few years in prison, considering what the rest of us went through?"

"You're right." Cece decided the only hope she and Sierra had of surviving this big confession was to play along. To get as much information as possible. "I have no right to complain. What about that man? The one who started all this with our mother? If she hadn't cheated, maybe our father wouldn't have turned into such a monster. This is all her fault."

"He paid for his sins," Marcus assured her. "He was every bit as evil as our father. He didn't deserve to live, either. They both were sent to hell where they belonged."

Cece took Sierra by the hand and then reached for her brother's. "We are all we have left. Us and Levi. We should make a pact to take care of each other. God knows our parents didn't."

Marcus stared at her for a long moment. "You shouldn't have come back, Cece. You're not like us." He looked to Sierra then. "You know what has to happen."

Cece shifted her attention to Sierra.

"He's right," her sister said. "I tried to help you and now it's too late. You shouldn't have come back, Cece."

DEACON WAS THROUGH WAITING. If Tanner didn't arrive soon with that warrant and backup, he was going in alone.

Still no movement at the house. They could be doing anything in there. It had been better than three hours since he saw Cece leaving. He wasn't waiting any longer. His cell vibrated. Deacon snatched it from his pocket and answered.

"Where are you?" the caller demanded.

*Tanner.*

"I'm at the edge of the woods near the house. Did you get the warrant?"

"I'm coming in."

The call ended. Damn it. Why didn't he just answer the question?

Deacon waited for Tanner to reach his position. Two of his deputies were right behind him. "Do you have the warrant?"

"The judge was in court. We should have his signature any minute."

"That's a no," Deacon snapped. "I'm not waiting."

Tanner started to argue with him but reached for his ringing cell phone, instead. Deacon waited, hoped it was the warrant.

"Got it. Thanks." He tucked his phone away. "Warrant's been signed." He looked to his deputies. "Call it."

While the deputies took care of notifying the rest of the team Tanner already had in place that it was time to get moving, he and Deacon headed directly for the house.

No vehicles had arrived during the time Deacon had been watching. At the front door, Tanner did the knocking. After three attempts to get someone to the door, he went in, gun drawn.

They moved quickly from room to room, first and second floor. No sign of anyone. Then they looked in the basement. One large brick-floored-and-walled room. Empty beyond a few jars of canned goods and a couple of boxes that had been stored long enough to look vintage.

"No one came in or out of the house while I was watching," Deacon said, frustrated.

"Marcus and a couple of his followers are over at the

church. My deputies should be finished going through the building by now." He reached for his cell.

"Wait. Did you say Marcus was there?"

Tanner nodded. "He is."

Deacon turned all the way around in the basement. "Then there has to be an underground tunnel because he was in this house and he did not leave by either of the exits."

They started with the walls, going over every square inch in hopes of finding a hidden passageway. They moved on to the floors. Nothing.

"Let's go back to the first floor," Tanner suggested.

Upstairs the deputies were moving through the house, looking for the shotgun Tanner had listed on his warrant. They went through each room, finally entering the only first floor bedroom, which obviously belonged to Marcus. Male clothes were in the closet. They moved the rug on the floor, the furniture, and found nothing.

Back in the closet, Deacon checked the floorboards. "Got something here," he said to Tanner.

A square of flooring lifted up, revealing a trapdoor. A metal ladder led downward into the darkness.

"I'm going first," Tanner said in no uncertain terms.

As much as Deacon would have liked to argue, the sheriff was right. This was his jurisdiction. Deacon followed, moving down slowly and as soundlessly as possible. When they reached the bottom of the ladder, Tanner used his cell as a flashlight and discovered a light switch. He turned it on, revealing a long tunnel lined with doors.

"What the hell?" Tanner muttered.

One by one they checked behind the doors and found nothing. Midway along the tunnel were two doors that were locked. When they couldn't get an answer from beyond the locked doors, Tanner left two deputies attempting to open them while he and Deacon moved on. At the other end of the tunnel was another ladder. Tanner went up first. He raised the trapdoor carefully and climbed on out. Deacon did the same.

The room they found themselves in was small. Hooks for coats lined three of the four walls. The one window looked out onto the woods. They were at the church.

*Voices.*

Tanner moved to the door. Indicated for Deacon to keep quiet.

He listened a moment longer, then stepped back and prepared to open the door. Deacon leveled his weapon, ready to fire if necessary.

Beyond the door was the main worship hall of the church.

Marcus Winters, his sister Sierra and two other men looked up from the books they held.

"What is this?" Marcus shot to his feet.

"Where is Cece?" Tanner demanded.

Deacon moved through the room, went down a small hall behind the stage-like pulpit and checked both bathrooms.

Nothing.

Sweat broke out across his forehead. His pulse rate climbed higher and higher. She had to be here.

Marcus was arguing with Tanner about his sister.

"We haven't spoken in years," Marcus was saying.

The two older men sat silent, watching. Sierra stared at the floor or the book she held, presumably a Bible.

Tanner continued to pressure Marcus. Deacon zeroed in on Sierra.

"Where is she, Sierra?"

Sierra lifted her gaze to his.

"Don't allow him to intimidate you, sister!" Marcus shouted.

Tanner told him to shut up.

"Where is Cece?" Deacon pressed, moving closer to her.

"She's gone to be with the *others*."

Fear knotted in Deacon's belly. "Can you show me how to find where she is?"

Marcus started to yell again and Tanner pushed him into a chair and shoved his weapon into Marcus's face. "Not another word."

"Please," Deacon urged. "Show me where she is before it's too late."

He had no idea what kind of place she meant, but he innately understood it was not good.

She nodded and tossed the book aside.

Marcus dared to threaten her once more but Sierra didn't look back. Deacon stayed right on her heels. She went out the back of the church. By the time they reached the tree line, two deputies had joined them.

As they moved into the trees, Sierra hurried faster and faster. Deacon sensed her anticipation and her fear.

A half mile or so into the thick woods, Sierra stopped. Deacon held up a hand for those behind them to stop.

She pointed. "There."

Cece was tied to a tree, a gag preventing her from screaming.

Deacon started around Sierra. She put a hand on his arm. "Be careful. The *others* could be out there."

Deacon looked to one of the deputies. "Don't let her out of your sight."

"Yes, sir," the deputy agreed.

Deacon and the other deputy moved forward. The deputy kept watch while Deacon went to Cece. He removed the gag of tape and cloth first. She cried out.

"I've got you," he assured her.

The deputy had a knife and cut loose her bindings. Cece fell against Deacon, nearly too weak to walk.

"We have to get out of here," she whispered.

He grabbed her up in his arms and started back in the direction from which they had come. The deputy who had stayed with Sierra escorted her while the third brought up the rear, keeping watch.

When they reached the church, several more squad cars had arrived. Marcus had been arrested, as had the two followers who had been at the church with him.

When Deacon lowered Cece to her feet, she turned to her sister. "Thank you."

Sierra nodded.

Cece put her hand on her arm. "It's time to tell the truth now."

# Chapter Fifteen

*Thursday, August 8*

Wednesday had passed in a blur of jurisdictional issues and frustration for Deacon. Marcus Winters had given Jack Kemp to these so-called *others* to ensure he never got the truth out of Sierra.

According to Sierra, no one knew who the *others* were. Deacon figured the whole story was something Marcus had made up to keep his sister in line. The Bureau had authorized ground-penetrating radar since there was a strong possibility there would be more remains than Jack's found somewhere on the Winters property.

One of the followers who was in the church with Marcus when the warrant was served had decided to help with the investigation for a chance at immunity. It was too early to say how much help his assistance would prove to be.

Cece had asked to stay with her sister while she gave her statement. Tanner had agreed. Which gave Deacon an opportunity to sit in on the questioning of Benton

Syler, the follower who had agreed to cooperate with the investigation.

"Mason kept a tight lid on how he operated. Marcus worked a little more loosely with a couple of us."

"Mr. Syler," Tanner asked, "can we anticipate finding human remains buried on the church property?"

Syler nodded. "There's plenty. The killings go way back. As for Kemp, I don't know anything about him. That was a personal matter between Marcus and Sierra. It wasn't decided by the council."

Deacon wanted to reach across the interview table and shake the hell out of the man. They had learned that the council was a group of four followers who made decisions, with Marcus leading.

"Did the council make life-and-death decisions on a regular basis?"

Tanner didn't do a very good job of hiding his disgust when he asked that question. Syler noticed.

"I was only ever in on three. Not because I wanted to be but because I did as I was told, sheriff. I didn't want my family to end up on the agenda."

"Are you suggesting Marcus would have harmed your family if you didn't follow his lead?"

"I'm not suggesting anything, sheriff. I'm telling you that's the way it was. Don't get me wrong. I worked hard to get this position. I figured my family and I were safer if I was in a higher position. No surprises that way."

It never ceased to amaze Deacon how far one man would go to please another when it came to societal hierarchy.

"Most of our decisions were about who would be

handed over to the *others* if they did wrong. I think the three who were stoned to death had something to do with a bad thing that happened to Marcus when he was a kid. But I don't know for sure and I knew better than to ask."

Sierra had said that Cece was to be given to the *others*. "Who do you mean?" Deacon asked.

Syler looked at him as if he wasn't sure whether he should answer. Tanner gave him a nod and he proceeded.

"The *others* are the most extreme wing of the Resurrection, an offshoot. Went off on their own years ago. We're talking way over the edge. Human sacrifices. You name it. Back when Mason first started the church, we had a couple of members go missing. Their mangled or cleaned-to-the-bone remains would show up eventually. Mason sent men into the woods looking for what he expected to be wild animals. Bears or mountain lions. Something like that. What he found was this extreme group. He figured out the only way to keep them from hunting among his followers was to supply them with what they wanted."

"You can lead us to these *others*?" Tanner asked.

"No one knows where they are. You mess around in those woods long enough and they'll find you."

A knock at the door sounded before one of Tanner's deputies came in. She whispered something in the sheriff's ear and hurried back out of the room.

Tanner stood. "Mr. Syler, we'll need to continue this at a later time. I have an emergency to see to."

Deacon followed Tanner out of the interview room. "What's going on?"

"The second warrant, that allowed us a more liberal search," he explained, "has found something I think your friends at the FBI and at the ATF will be interested in."

"Weapons?"

Tanner nodded. "A whole load hidden in that tunnel. I'm guessing Marcus was using the church as a neutral holding ground between the dealers and the Resurrection members."

"Sheriff." Another deputy hustled toward them. "You're going to want to come and listen to what Sierra Winters is saying about her brother Levi."

Deacon and Tanner followed the deputy to the observation room.

"Run that interview back," Tanner ordered the technician who was recording the interview.

"Right there," the deputy said.

The tech hit Play.

"Levi was working with Jack. He was helping him get in with the Resurrection. Until Jack figured out I was his daughter and then he got distracted."

Deacon's instincts moved to a higher level of alert.

"I think Levi has lingered on the fringes of those crazy preppers all this time. He's been very secretive about where he goes when he disappears for a few days. I believe that's where he is now. I don't know if they've figured out he's trying to bring them down or if they like him and want him in deeper. Either way, he's playing with fire. Those people don't play games."

The worry on Cece's face made Deacon's gut clench. He walked out of the observation booth and made a phone call. There was only one way this could end even remotely well.

He intended to do all he could to see that Levi was brought back alive.

For Cece. For Jack's family.

Levi would know more about Jack's last days than anyone else.

BY THE TIME the district attorney was finished interviewing Sierra, Cece was exhausted. Her head was still reeling at the idea of what her older brother had done. Dear God, what her father had done.

He had killed their mother. He had castrated his own son.

How the hell were any of them supposed to get past this?

Sierra would be in protective custody for now, so Cece gave her a hug before parting ways.

She had known her father was a cruel, evil man, but she had had no idea just how depraved he had been. The district attorney had assured Cece that the charge against her would be overturned. She could start her life over with a clean slate. She had been waiting to hear those words for most of her adult life.

In the corridor outside the sheriff's office, Deacon waited, one shoulder leaned against the wall as if he had been watching for her.

She smiled. Thankful to see him again. There was

so much she needed to say to him. So much she wanted to ask him.

Mostly she wanted him to know she was very grateful.

"Hey." He searched her eyes as if unsure how to proceed.

"Hey." She smiled. "I am glad to see you."

His lips stretched into a matching smile. "I can't tell you how happy I am to hear that."

"We have a lot to talk about," she confessed.

He nodded. "We do."

"I'm really worried about Levi."

"You have every right to be," he agreed. "The good news is, I made a call. The best retrieval expert in the Bureau has agreed to help find Levi."

Hope lit in Cece's chest. "That's great news. How soon will the agent be here?"

"She's on the way. She'll be here by morning. Her name is Sadie Buchanan. She's the best extraction and recovery agent in this part of the country. If anyone can find him and bring him home, it's Sadie."

"The district attorney says Sierra won't be charged. It was self-defense. She'll need therapy." Cece laughed. "I guess we all will. We Winters are pretty screwed up." She searched Deacon's gaze. "I know Marcus has a lot to answer for and he'll likely spend the rest of his life locked away somewhere, but he was a victim, too, and I'm sorry no one recognized it in time to save him."

Deacon touched her cheek. "At least he can't hurt anyone else or himself. He'll be on a different path now."

"I'm tired." Another raw confession. "Will you take me home?"

"I will."

Cece wrapped her arm around his and leaned against his shoulder. When they were outside and headed across the parking lot to his truck, she pulled him to a stop and stared up into his brown eyes. "I can't leave Winchester until we find Levi and I know Sierra will be okay. But I want to know you better, Deacon Ross."

"I'll be right here with you, Cece Winters. I can't think of anything I would rather do than get better acquainted."

She went up on her tiptoes, put her arms around his neck and kissed him on the lips. She had spent too long waiting for her life to begin again. She had no intention of wasting another minute.

\* \* \* \* \*

*Don't miss the next Winchester,
Tennessee Thriller,* The Safest Lies,
*coming next month from Debra Webb and
Harlequin Intrigue!*

*Read on for an excerpt!*

# Chapter One

*Winchester, Tennessee*
*Friday, August 9*

Sadie Buchanan had never been to Winchester before. The closest she'd come was Tullahoma and that
had been years ago when she was first assigned to the
Nashville area. A joint task force conference at the Ar-
nold Air Force Base had required her attendance for
a day. Frankly, it was unusual for an agent to end up
in this area, much less request a retrieval. The kind of
trouble that required her participation rarely happened
in small towns. Most of her assignments took her to
the larger metropolitan areas around the state or deep
in the desert or the mountains.

In any event, whenever an agent was in trouble,
she went in.

She parked in front of the Franklin County sheriff's
office. Extracting agents from dangerous situations
hadn't exactly been a part of her plan when she started her
career, but within two years of her first field assignment
she found herself doing exactly that after one particular

mission. The assignment, as well as the agent involved, had been high profile, garnering her the full attention of the powers that be. During that fateful mission she, as well as the Bureau, discovered her knack for getting in and out with particular ease. From that point forward, she had been focused on training for moments like this one. It wasn't the sort of task just any agent felt comfortable doing. Success required a very particular skill set.

Go in. Attain the target. Get out alive.

Her father always said that everyone had a gift. Evidently, this was hers. It hadn't failed her yet. She had no intention of allowing it to start today.

Inside the brick building that housed the sheriff's department and county jail, a female desk sergeant greeted her.

"Special Agent Sadie Buchanan." Sadie showed her credentials to the other woman. "I'm here to see Sheriff Tanner and Agent Ross."

"Good morning, Agent Buchanan. Down the hall and to the left," Sergeant Rodriquez said with a gesture toward the long corridor beyond her desk. "They're waiting for you in the conference room, ma'am."

Sadie thanked the sergeant and headed in the direction indicated. One thing she had noticed about Winchester already—and it was barely ten o'clock in the morning—it was a couple of degrees hotter than Nashville. The town was attractive in a quaint sort of way, on the shores of a lake and bordered by hills and woods. Most folks would see those hills and woods as nature's perfect landscape. What Sadie saw in all that natural beauty were places to hide. Lots and lots of potential hiding places.

Not a good thing when attempting to locate a target.

She opened the door to the conference room and walked in. Four people waited for her but only one she recognized: Special Agent Deacon Ross. He, too, was assigned to Nashville. They'd only worked together on one occasion, but he had a stellar reputation. The last she'd heard he had taken an extended leave of absence.

Maybe the rumors that he might not be coming back were just that—rumors. He certainly appeared to be involved in this case.

"Agent Buchanan," a tall, dark-haired man at the head of the table said as he stood, "I'm Sheriff Colt Tanner. We're glad you could come." He extended his hand.

Sadie gave his hand a shake. "Happy to help, sheriff."

"This is Chief of Police Billy Brannigan." Tanner gestured to another man; this one had brown hair and eyes and looked as much like a cowboy as the sheriff did.

Brannigan extended his hand across the conference table. "Good to meet you, Agent Buchanan."

"Likewise, chief." Sadie accepted the gesture and turned to the next man in the room. "Agent Ross." She offered her hand.

Ross gave her hand a shake and then turned to the woman at his side. "This is Cecelia Winters."

Sadie reached her hand out once more, this time toward the petite woman with the fiery mane of red hair. "Ms. Winters."

Winters brushed her palm briefly against Sadie's

but didn't speak. Since she had the same last name as the target, Sadie assumed she was a wife or other family member.

"Why don't we have a seat and get started?" Ross suggested.

Sadie pulled out a chair and sat down as the others resumed their seats. A couple of files and a stack of maps lay on the table. Not exactly the typical setup for a tactical mission briefing, but she'd gotten the impression this one was different than her usual assignment. She didn't have a problem with different. As long as it didn't get anyone killed. Sadie had yet to lose a target once she had identified him or her.

"I imagine," Ross said, "you were briefed on the situation we have."

"I only just returned to Nashville late last night from an assignment in Memphis. I'm afraid the details I received are sketchy, at best. I was under the impression I would be fully briefed when I arrived."

This would certainly be her first briefing with a civilian present who was totally unrelated to the official aspects of the investigation. She had a feeling this assignment was going to become more and more unusual.

"A particular group of extremists in the Franklin County area was pinpointed more than two decades ago. Gunrunning was suspected to be a major part of this group's activities. Over the past few years suspicions of their involvement with kidnapping, possibly related to human trafficking, have surfaced. My former partner, Jack Kemp, investigated this group when it was first discovered but at the time there was not enough substantial evidence that the members were involved in anything criminal or illegal to warrant any sort of operation. Just over nine years ago that status changed, and Jack came back for a second look. During the course of that assignment he disappeared. Recently, new information about what happened to him has come to light. In part, that information was obtained through a civilian informant. Like most of us, Jack worked with a number of civilians."

"One of those informants was Levi Winters," Sheriff Tanner added. "Levi has recently gone missing and we suspect this group may be involved."

Brannigan didn't add anything. Sadie was undecided as to whether his continued silence was a good thing. Perhaps his involvement was only for informational purposes. The target was likely outside his official jurisdiction.

"Is the Bureau opening a new case in the area?" Seemed a no-brainer. But Sadie was not up to speed on the happenings in Franklin County. The more Ross talked, the more she understood that he had friends in high places and that was why she was here. "Or is this one off the record?"

The men in the room exchanged a look, which answered the question without anyone having to say a word.

"To a degree," Ross admitted, "the retrieval is off the record. There appears to be some hesitation about reopening the case involving the group known as Resurrection. We're hoping any information Levi may have will help make that happen."

Making it doubly important that she brought him

back alive. Sadie considered the other woman at the table. The hope in her eyes was impossible to miss. Right now, Sadie could walk away and that decision would not adversely affect her career since this mission was off the record. She could stand up, walk out that door and never look back rather than risk her life for some informant she did not know.

Chances were, if she made that decision, the informant would die.

And though that decision would not prove unfavorable to her career, it would prove immensely unfavorable to her conscience.

"I see. Let's have a look at what I'm up against."

Tanner went first. He explained that he had not encountered any trouble with members of this group—at least, none of which he was aware. The members of the so-called Resurrection group were anonymous. Any who lived in the community kept quiet about their involvement. Neighbors, friends, possibly even family had no idea about their participation. The tactic was actually fairly common and had been used for centuries by one secret group or another.

Brannigan spoke for the first time, agreeing with Tanner's summation. The Winchester Police Department had not run into trouble with anyone who claimed to be or who was thought to be involved with this extreme group. The crime rate in the county was comparatively low. Rumors regarding the group known as Resurrection leaned toward the idea of extreme or doomsday-type preppers. The problem was, there appeared to be an offshoot fringe group known only as the *others* who were far more dangerous.

Ross took over from there. "We've contacted a source within the ATF but we don't have anything back from them just yet. Whatever else we do, we can't keep waiting and risk losing Winters. Ultimately, the hope is that the Bureau and the ATF will initiate a joint task force, along with local law enforcement, to look more thoroughly into what this group is up to. For now, our immediate focus is on extracting Winters."

Sadie understood perfectly. "If Resurrection or this offshoot group has him, we need to get their attention. Obviously…" she scanned the faces at the table "…you don't have the location where he's being held."

Tanner tapped the stacks of maps. "There are certain areas we feel are the more likely places."

"But there's no time to search." Sadie nodded. "Time is our primary enemy." She set her gaze on Ross's, knowing he would understand the goal. "We need their attention. I would recommend a news bulletin about a missing federal agent last seen in the Winchester area. Keep it ambiguous for obvious reasons. Give my description but not my name." She shifted her attention to Tanner. "I'll start with the most likely place and beat the bushes until they find me."

"You want them to find you?" Tanner looked uneasy as he asked the question.

"We don't have time to locate and infiltrate any other way. Prompting them to find me will be much faster and far more efficient."

"Isn't that far more dangerous, as well?" Brannigan asked.

"Yes." Sadie saw no point in whitewashing the answer. "But it's the only way to accomplish our goal in a timely manner."

"Agent Buchanan is highly trained for exactly these sorts of situations," Ross assured all present.

Judging by the expressions Tanner and Brannigan wore, his assurance did little to alleviate their reservations.

"You're suggesting going in without backup." Brannigan shook his head. "The only thing I see coming of that is two hostages needing extraction."

Sadie acknowledged his assessment with a nod. "That is a possibility. But, chief, you can trust me when I say that if I wasn't experienced and completely confident in this situation, we wouldn't be having this conversation. I know what I'm doing. I understand the risk and I am not overly concerned."

"I may be able to help."

All gathered around the table turned to the woman who had spoken. Cecelia Winters looked directly at Sadie even as the men in the room started to argue with her announcement.

"Not happening," Ross stated unconditionally, tension in his voice, his posture and the set of his jaw.

"He's right," Tanner agreed with a firm shake of his head.

"This whole thing is far too risky as it is," Brannigan added.

Sadie ignored them all. Instead, she focused on the woman who had made the statement. "How do you believe you can help?"

Cecelia blinked at Sadie's question. "The people

in this town know me. They know what happened to me—to my family. Nothing is secret anymore. If I spread the news, they'll believe me. They will pass it along far more quickly than something reported in the news. Not everyone around here trusts the news."

"Cece," Ross argued, "you getting involved could only complicate matters."

Sadie got the picture now. Ross and Cecelia were a couple. He didn't want her anywhere near the line of fire. A personal connection more often than not spelled trouble when it came to an assignment like this one.

"Help from most any source can be useful, but Ross could be right," Sadie said, not to change the woman's mind but because it was true.

The hard look Ross sent her way shouted loud and clear that he wasn't happy with how she had responded to the offer. Too bad. He wanted Sadie to do a job, an extraction—a very risky extraction. Why wouldn't she use any available resources?

"Levi is my brother," Cecelia said. "I want to help." She glanced at Ross. "I need to help."

"You understand that when this is over, there could be a backlash?" Sadie needed her to comprehend the long-range ramifications of any step she might opt to take. Sadie didn't like getting civilians involved but it seemed as if this one was already eyeball deep in the situation.

"I do. The past decade of my life has been one long backlash. I think I can handle a little more."

Ross obviously didn't think so.

Sadie stared directly at him. "Is this going to be a problem for you?"

She didn't like problems. Especially those that came from the people who were supposed to be on her side.

He held her gaze for a moment before saying, "I guess not."

"Good." Sadie turned back to Cecelia. "You tell whomever you believe will get the word out the fastest that the agent who was working with your brother showed up and was going around town asking questions." She shrugged. "Trying to help, but now she's suddenly gone missing and you're worried about her."

Cecelia nodded. "Okay. I can do that."

"The most likely starting place?" Sadie asked, looking from one man to the next.

"The church," Ross said. He glanced at Cecelia as he spoke. "We have reason to believe the Salvation Survivalists were working with the primary group in some capacity. They were housing weapons most likely intended for Resurrection, but we don't have solid evidence of that conclusion. The ATF is looking at that possibility along with numerous others but they're taking too damned long and they're not sharing."

"But you're certain the two are or were connected."

"We are," Ross said.

Tanner and Brannigan agreed, as well.

"Then that's where I'll start." To Cecelia she said, "You put the word out about me asking questions." She shifted her attention to Tanner. "Make sure the local news reports a missing federal agent. No name, just a description."

Tanner nodded. "I can make that happen."

"I'd like to familiarize myself with maps of the area, particularly around the church."

Ross spread the maps on the conference table and started the briefing regarding the landscape. Sadie took her time and carefully committed the maps to memory. One of the things that made her good at her job was her ability to memorize maps and recall landmarks. For a girl who grew up in the city, she was a damned good tracker. As good as any hunter she'd ever worked with and she'd worked with a few.

More than anything, she paid attention. The old saying that it was all in the details was true more often than not. The details were crucial. She didn't need a photographic memory to recall the details. She just had to pay attention.

"What about the church?" Sadie considered the map of the area around the church, which appeared to be well outside town. "I need some additional history on it."

"My father started the church about thirty-five years ago," Cecelia explained. "He was a very cruel man, capable of anything. He had—has—many devoted followers who turned to my older brother, Marcus, after our father's death. There are those who still believe one or both to be messiahs of a sort. I'm confident the most deeply devoted know far more than they've shared. If they hear about you, I'm confident the word will go where you want it."

Ross pushed a folder in Sadie's direction. "This will give you a good overview of what we know. It's not complete by any means, but it's as much as anyone knows."

Sadie opened the file and skimmed the first page. "I'd like some time to go over what you have and then I'll drive out to the church, hide my car and start digging around. If I'm lucky, someone will come looking for me in short order."

"For the record," Chief of Police Brannigan spoke up, "I still think this is a bad idea."

Sadie wished she could convince him otherwise, but to an extent he was correct. This was most likely a bad idea.

But their options were limited. Sometimes the bad ideas were the only feasible ones.

# INTRIGUE

## Available August 20, 2019

### #1875 TANGLED THREAT
by Heather Graham
Years ago, FBI agent Brock McGovern was arrested for a crime he didn't commit. Now that he's been cleared of all charges, he'll do whatever it takes to find the culprit. With two women missing, Brock's ex-girlfriend Maura Antrium is eager to help him. Can they find the killer...or will he find them first?

### #1876 FULL FORCE
*Declan's Defenders* • by Elle James
After working at the Russian embassy in Washington, DC, Emily Chastain is targeted by a relentless killer. When she calls upon Declan's Defenders in order to find someone to help her, former Force Recon marine Frank "Mustang" Ford vows to find the person who is threatening her.

### #1877 THE SAFEST LIES
*A Winchester, Tennessee Thriller* • by Debra Webb
Special Agent Sadie Buchanen is deep in the backcountry of Winchester, Tennessee, in order to retrieve a hostage taken by a group of extreme survivalists. When she finds herself in danger, she must rely on Smith Flynn, an intriguing stranger who is secretly an undercover ATF special agent.

### #1878 MURDERED IN CONARD COUNTY
*Conard County: The Next Generation* • by Rachel Lee
When a man is killed, Blaire Afton and Gus Maddox, two park rangers, must team up to find the murderer. Suddenly, they discover they are after a serial killer... But can they stop him before he claims another victim?

### #1879 CONSTANT RISK
*The Risk Series: A Bree and Tanner Thriller* • by Janie Crouch
A serial killer is loose in Dallas, and only Bree Daniels and Tanner Dempsey can stop him. With bodies piling up around them, can they find the murderer before more women die?

### #1880 WANTED BY THE MARSHAL
*American Armor* • by Ryshia Kennie
After nurse Kiera Connell is abducted by a serial killer and barely escapes with her life, she must rely on US marshal Travis Johnson's protection. But while Travis believes the murderer is in jail, Kiera knows a second criminal is on the loose and eager to silence her.

---

**YOU CAN FIND MORE INFORMATION ON UPCOMING HARLEQUIN® TITLES, FREE EXCERPTS AND MORE AT WWW.HARLEQUIN.COM.**

HICNM0819

# Get 4 FREE REWARDS!

## We'll send you 2 FREE Books
## plus 2 FREE Mystery Gifts.

**Harlequin Intrigue®** books feature heroes and heroines that confront and survive danger while finding themselves irresistibly drawn to one another.

**FREE**
Value Over
**$20**

---

**YES!** Please send me 2 FREE Harlequin Intrigue® novels and my 2 FREE gifts (gifts are worth about $10 retail). After receiving them, if I don't wish to receive any more books, I can return the shipping statement marked "cancel." If I don't cancel, I will receive 6 brand-new novels every month and be billed just $4.99 each for the regular-print edition or $5.99 each for the larger-print edition in the U.S., or $5.74 each for the regular-print edition or $6.49 each for the larger-print edition in Canada. That's a savings of at least 12% off the cover price! It's quite a bargain! Shipping and handling is just 50¢ per book in the U.S. and $1.25 per book in Canada.* I understand that accepting the 2 free books and gifts places me under no obligation to buy anything. I can always return a shipment and cancel at any time. The free books and gifts are mine to keep no matter what I decide.

Choose one:  ☐ **Harlequin Intrigue®**      ☐ **Harlequin Intrigue®**
                  **Regular-Print**              **Larger-Print**
                  (182/382 HDN GNXC)            (199/399 HDN GNXC)

Name (please print)

Address                                                                 Apt. #

City                           State/Province                    Zip/Postal Code

Mail to the **Reader Service:**
**IN U.S.A.:** P.O. Box 1341, Buffalo, NY 14240-8531
**IN CANADA:** P.O. Box 603, Fort Erie, Ontario L2A 5X3

Want to try 2 free books from another series? Call 1-800-873-8635 or visit www.ReaderService.com.

---

*Terms and prices subject to change without notice. Prices do not include sales taxes, which will be charged (if applicable) based on your state or country of residence. Canadian residents will be charged applicable taxes. Offer not valid in Quebec. This offer is limited to one order per household. Books received may not be as shown. Not valid for current subscribers to Harlequin Intrigue books. All orders subject to approval. Credit or debit balances in a customer's account(s) may be offset by any other outstanding balance owed by or to the customer. Please allow 4 to 6 weeks for delivery. Offer available while quantities last.

**Your Privacy**—The Reader Service is committed to protecting your privacy. Our Privacy Policy is available online at www.ReaderService.com or upon request from the Reader Service. We make a portion of our mailing list available to reputable third parties that offer products we believe may interest you. If you prefer that we not exchange your name with third parties, or if you wish to clarify or modify your communication preferences, please visit us at www.ReaderService.com/consumerschoice or write to us at Reader Service Preference Service, P.O. Box 9062, Buffalo, NY 14240-9062. Include your complete name and address.

HI19R3

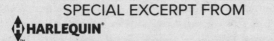
"I've been assigned to go back to Florida. To stay at the Frampton Ranch and Resort—and investigate what we believe to be three kidnappings and a murder. And the kidnappings may have nothing to do with the resort, nor may the murder?" Brock McGovern asked, a small note of incredulity slipping into his voice, which was surprising to him—he was always careful to keep an even tone.

FBI assistant director Richard Egan had brought him into his office, and Brock had known he was going on assignment—he just hadn't expected this.

"Yes, not what you'd want, but, hey, maybe it'll be good for you—and perhaps necessary now, when time is of the essence and there is no one out there who could know the place or the circumstances with the same scope and experience you have," Egan told him. "Three young women have disappeared from the area. Two of them were guests of the Frampton Ranch and Resort shortly before their disappearances—the third had left St. Augustine and was on her way there. The Florida Department of Law Enforcement has naturally been there already. They asked for federal help on this. Shades of the past haunt them—they don't want any more unsolved murders—and everyone is hoping against hope that Lily Sylvester, Amy Bonham and Lydia Merkel might be found."

"These are Florida missing-person cases," Brock said. "And it's sad but true that young people go to Florida and get caught up in the beach life and the club scene. And regrettable but true once again—there's a drug and alcohol culture that does exist and people get caught up in it. Not just in Florida, of course, but everywhere." He smiled grimly. "I go where I'm told, but I'm curious—how is this an FBI affair? And forgive me, but—FBI out of New York?"

"Not out of New York. FDLE asked for you. Specifically."

*Don't miss*
Tangled Threat *by Heather Graham,*
*available September 2019 wherever*
*Harlequin® books and ebooks are sold.*

www.Harlequin.com

Need an adrenaline rush from nail-biting tales
(and irresistible males)?

Check out **Harlequin Intrigue®**,
**Harlequin® Romantic Suspense** and
**Love Inspired® Suspense** books!

## New books available every month!

### CONNECT WITH US AT:

Facebook.com/groups/HarlequinConnection

 Facebook.com/HarlequinBooks

 Twitter.com/HarlequinBooks

 Instagram.com/HarlequinBooks

Pinterest.com/HarlequinBooks

ReaderService.com

**ROMANCE WHEN
YOU NEED IT**

SGENRE2018R

Another scream rose in her throat as the icy water rushed in around her. She fought to free herself, but the ropes that bound her wrists to the steering wheel held tight, chafing her skin until it tore and bled. Her throat was raw from screaming, while outside the car, the wind kicked up whitecaps on the pond. The waves lapped at the windows. Inside the car, water rose around her feet, before climbing up her legs to lap at her waist.

She pleaded for help as the water began to rise up to her chest. But anyone who might have helped her was back at the high school graduation party she'd just left. If only she'd stayed at the party. If only she hadn't burned so many bridges earlier tonight. If only…

As the water lapped against her throat, she screamed even though she knew no one was coming to her rescue. Certainly not the person standing on the shore watching.

The pond was outside of town, away from everything. She knew now that was why her killer had chosen it. Worse, no one would be looking for her, not after the way she'd behaved when she'd left the party.

"You're big on torturing people," her killer had said. "Not so much fun when the shoe is on the other foot, huh?"

More than half-drunk, the bitter taste of betrayal in her mouth, she'd wanted to beg for her life. But her pride wouldn't let her. As her hands were bound to the steering wheel, she tried to convince herself that the only reason this was happening was to scare her. No one would actually kill her. Not even someone she'd bullied at school.

She was Ariel Matheson. Everyone wanted to be her friend. Everyone wanted to be her, sexy spoiled rich girl. No one hated her enough to go through with this. Even when the car had been pushed into the pond, she told herself that her new baby blue SUV wouldn't sink. Or if it did, the water wouldn't be deep enough that she'd drown.

The dank water splashed into her face. Frantic, she tried to sit up higher, but the seat belt and the rope on her wrists held her down. The car lurched under her as it wallowed almost full of water on the rough surface of the pond. Waves washed over the windshield, obscuring the lights of Whitefish, Montana, as the SUV slowly began to sink and she felt the last few minutes of her life slipping away.

She spit out a mouthful and told herself that this wasn't happening. Things like this didn't happen to her. This was not the way her life would end. It couldn't be.

Panic made her suck in another mouthful of awful-tasting water. She tried to hold her breath as she told herself that she was destined for so much more. The girl most likely to end up with everything she wanted, it said in her yearbook.

Bubbles rose around her as the car filled to the headliner, forcing her to let out the breath she'd been holding. This was real. This wasn't just to scare her.

The last thing she saw before the SUV sank the rest of the way was her killer standing on the bank in the dark night, watching her die. Would anyone miss her? Mourn her? She'd made so many enemies. Would anyone even come looking for her in the days ahead? Her parents would think that she'd run away. Her friends…

Fury replaced her fear. They thought she was a bitch before? As water filled her lungs, she swore that if she had it to do over, she'd make them all pay.

*Don't miss*
**Just His Luck** *by B.J. Daniels,*
*available September 2019 wherever*
*Harlequin® books and ebooks are sold.*

**www.Harlequin.com**

# *Love Harlequin romance?*

## DISCOVER.

Be the first to find out about promotions,
news and exclusive content!

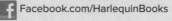 Facebook.com/HarlequinBooks

Twitter.com/HarlequinBooks

Instagram.com/HarlequinBooks

Pinterest.com/HarlequinBooks

ReaderService.com

## EXPLORE.

Sign up for the Harlequin e-newsletter and
download a free book from any series at
**TryHarlequin.com.**

## CONNECT.

Join our Harlequin community to share
your thoughts and connect with other
romance readers!
**Facebook.com/groups/HarlequinConnection**

 **HARLEQUIN®**

**ROMANCE WHEN
YOU NEED IT**